Heartstrings & HOLIDAYS

WILLA KAY

Heartstrings & Holidays

Oak Ridge Book 1.5

Willa Kay

To the ones who thought the first book was too spicy,
I have terrible news for you. It starts in Chapter 3.
Merry Christmas, and you're welcome.

Content Warnings & Introductions

Warning: this book contains pure fluff with minimal plot and plenty of spice within its pages. I do recommend that you read Heartstrings & Horizons first before diving into the cozy small town of Oak Ridge for the holiday season.

There are multiple (8) POVs in the first part of this book, and that can be confusing to some readers, so I've compiled a list of our cast so you can get to know them a little bit if you haven't read book one.

Paige: Canadian, introvert, plus-size baddie, married to Cade. FMC of Heartstrings & Horizons

Cade: Homegrown Kentuckian, owner of The Ridge, down bad for his wife, Paige. MMC of Heartstrings & Horizons

Miles: Contractor, jokester, and golden retriever best friend to Cade. Maggie's nemesis.

Mags: American export currently living in Toronto. Paige's former roommate and bestie. Miles' wet dream and worst nightmare.

Ivy: Single mom to Rylin and artist. FMC of book two, coming soon!

Liam: Bartender at The Ridge and Cade's employee and good friend. Single dad to Aidan.

Dean: Rounding out the trip, best friend to Miles and Cade. In love with Cara.

Cara: Nurse and plus size baddie. In love with Dean.

Triggers: (spoiler warning)

Mention of past abusive relationship (off page)
Pregnancy & related symptoms (on page)
Sexually explicit content (in abundance)
Near death experience (brief and no harm done)

If you don't enjoy open door spice, this might not be the book for you and that's okay! But if you like your holiday novellas cozy, and your MCs filthy as fuck — you're welcome.

PART ONE

Mistletoe & MISCHIEF

Paige's Holiday Playlist

There are song titles accompanying every chapter.

Chapter 1

Prologue - Mags

🎵 It's Beginning to look a lot like Christmas - Michael Bublé

If I don't think about it too deeply, Christmas in Oak Ridge sounds like a dream. The scenic Kentucky town is beautiful, with all of its small town charm and cozy lakefront views. I've even grown to love the people there — not just my bestie. Though I *have* been missing having Paige as a roommate. Obviously, I'm thrilled she's found her soulmate, but I fucking miss her like a lost limb.

Despite my excitement, I'm also bracing myself for one very specific inevitability — I'll have to come face to face with the last person I ever want to see again: Miles Fucking Barlow — I'm sure that's not his actual middle name, but it fits. He could even hyphenate to Mother-Fucking for a little extra razzle dazzle.

My list of grievances with the aforementioned asshole is extensive, but I'm not quite ready to unpack all of that. If it weren't for the unfortunate fact that our best friends are married to each other, I would be perfectly happy to never see

1

him or hear his name ever again. So why the fuck does just the mere thought of him still give me butterflies?

"Passport — check. Secret Santa gift — I chuckle at this one — check. Snow gear — not likely to need it, but also check." It looks like everything is in order for my flight to Nashville, so I lock up my house in Toronto and head to the airport with my bags in tow. My dear old dad is flying out of Nashville International on his way to Aspen with his new girlfriend, so he's leaving one of his cars at the airport for me. I'll be able to make the short 90 minute drive to Oak Ridge in peace, preparing myself for my looming encounter with him.

The cabin is pretty big — surely we can keep our distance for a few hours. Rolling my eyes, I huff out a laugh. Who am I kidding? I'm staying in Oak Ridge for 2 weeks. There's no way my only run-in is going to be at Paige's Christmas party. You can do this, Mags.

Once my Uber pulls up to the airport, I head straight to the check-in counter. The whole process is a breeze, and I'm grateful when my luggage doesn't exceed the weight limit. It's a short three-hour flight to Nashville, but it's plenty of time to work on editing my next release: "Under the Mistletoe: A Cozy Holiday Novella" by M.W. Hartley. Nobody knows about my pen name, and I intend to keep it that way, so I'll have to keep my laptop tucked away for most of the trip.

It's not that I doubt my friends; I know Paige would be more supportive than anyone, but this was never part of the plan. I'm supposed to take over my dad's travel magazine when he retires. That's the whole reason I'm studying journalism in the first place. But writing romance — well, it's been an unexpected adventure. It started as an outlet when my university courses felt overwhelming, but now that I've self-published 2 romance novels, I just keep chasing the high. Love might not be in the cards for Maggie Watson — even if I once thought I had it within reach — but for M.W. Hartley, there's always a happily ever after.

Chapter 2

Cade

♫ *Christmas Tree Farm - Taylor Swift*

Snow in Oak Ridge, Kentucky is almost like the Cardinals beating the Wildcats to win the championship. I can count on one hand the number of white Christmases I've witnessed in my lifetime. So imagine my surprise when the local meteorologist, clad in his blue 3 piece suit adorned with snowmen announces that this week we'd see several inches of snowfall. The entire town is all up in arms, hunkering down for a rare Kentucky snowstorm. The local grocery shelves have been divested of their entire stock of milk and bread, and my wife is standing in the aisle, mouth agape, taking in the frenzy of shoppers. Her curves are downright sinful in her skin tight jeans, and red peacoat; curly hair haphazardly tucked under her black pom pom tipped beanie.

"Are y'all planning a French toast festival or something? What's with the milk and bread shortage?"

"Alright, Canada. Time for your first lesson about winter in Kentucky," I say with a smirk. "Kentuckians have no idea

4

how to handle snow. So, naturally, everybody panics, buys the most basic necessities, and holes up at home until it passes. Avoidance is in our DNA."

"Amateurs." She snorts out a laugh then saunters down the aisle towards the produce, securing everything to make loaded baked potatoes — her latest pregnancy craving.

"You're about to get an education, Cowboy. I'm totally making a holiday bucket list!"

Despite the urge to remind her she's supposed to be taking it easy because she's very much pregnant, I clamp my mouth shut. I've been hovering, and she's reminded me on several occasions to stop treating her like she's fragile. She made it very clear, in no uncertain terms, that she would be withholding certain privileges if I didn't "get my shit together" — her words, not mine — and I'm taking that threat very seriously.

"Ok, Sunshine. Let's grab this shit and get home before Mags arrives."

A look of excitement washes over her face at the mention of her best friend. Maggie's roommate is heading home for Christmas, and her dad is flying to Aspen with his girlfriend, which would've left Mags alone for the holidays. But Paige wasn't having it, so she invited Mags to spend Christmas at the cabin. It wasn't entirely unselfish; my girl has been missing her bestie.

30 minutes later, Paige hunches over the kitchen island with a pad of paper and a pen, her lip trapped between her teeth as she jots down her holiday bucket list.

"Ok. So. We're definitely going sledding. The hill down to the dock should have a decent drop as long as we stop before we get to the lake. We can make a wall at the bottom to prevent any unwanted polar plunging."

"And where do you propose we get sleds?" I ask, swiping a hand over my stubble.

"Already called Arch. He checked the stock room and found us a toboggan, a saucer, and a magic carpet, so we're set."

I furrow my brow in confusion. "How is a toboggan going to help?"

"You sit on it. Usually, it can hold a couple of people at a time."

"Paige... what do you think a toboggan is?"

"It's a wooden sled," she says matter-of-factly. When I frown in confusion, she continues. "Curved at the end with reins you can hold on to." Her hands fist the invisible rope, miming the act of sledding in a way that has me stifling a laugh. "What did you think it is?"

"In Kentucky, a toboggan is a winter hat," I explain.

"Wait, what? Like a toque?"

"What the hell is a toque?"

"A winter hat. I feel like we're talking in circles."

With an exasperated sigh, I wrap my arms around her shoulders, peeking at her list. "I'm gonna need a Canadian to American translator."

"Hi, I'm Paige. Nice to meet you," she says, turning on the stool to offer me a handshake. I grip her wrist and pull her to me, taking her mouth in a bruising kiss. She smiles against my lips as I pull back. "Love you," she whispers.

"Love you, more. So what else is on this list?"

"Building a snowman is mandatory. Snow angels, too. Oh! And a snowball fight!" Her face lights up as she continues down the list. I have no idea how we're going to manage it all before the snow melts, but if it puts that smile on her face, I'll do my damndest to make it all happen.

Paige

The once bare trees are now covered with a light dusting of snow as we walk down the center aisle of a small tree farm just outside of Oak Ridge. Our mitten clad hands are clasped between us as we search for the perfect tree. Earlier in the week, I received a huge care package from Nana, including all of my favorite snacks, and a matching set of hats and mitts for me and Cade. The chilly air is filled with the crisp scent of pine, and each step we take crunches underfoot, the sound echoing softly in the stillness around us.

I'm determined to have a picture perfect Christmas, and that includes my first ever real tree. We're cutting it a little close with only 8 days until Christmas, but Cade has been hovering over me like I might break, and my first busy season as a photographer kept me running around like a madwoman. After delivering the last gallery yesterday, I finally have time to soak in the season with my husband and all of our favorite people.

I lean closer, relishing the way Cade's shoulder brushes against mine, grounding me amid the flurry of excitement and my own swirling thoughts about the holidays.

"Oh! Look at this one!" I say, pointing to a very full, lush spruce that looks like it's straight out of a holiday card, with its symmetrical shape and rich green hue.

"Might be a bit big," Cade says, tilting his head to assess the size. "We'll need to make sure there's room for everyone in the den." His brow furrows as he considers our options, crinkling his eyes in that adorable way that makes my panties melt.

Tomorrow we'll be gathering at the cabin for our first annual Holiday Hoedown with the Elite 8: Mags, Miles, Liam, Dean, Cara, Ivy, me and Cade. It's not so much a hoedown as a Christmas party with a gift exchange, but I liked the alliteration. I've been planning the party for months, much to Cade's dismay. If it were up to him, he'd have me bubble wrapped and in bed 24/7. He thinks I'm working too hard, but it's just my default setting.

If I'm being honest, I think I enjoy planning parties because it gives me a sense of control, and I get to surround myself with my chosen family. Lord knows my real family left a lot to be desired over the years. I've had a lot of time to reflect on my past, and while it's hard to reconcile everything I've experienced with the person I am today, I'm determined to do things differently for my daughter. I know I can't shelter her from all the hurt in the world, but I refuse to be the direct cause of it.

With a nod, I tug Cade's hand, leading him to a row of smaller fir trees when a familiar voice sounds behind me.

"Fancy meeting you here."

"Mags! What are you doing here?" I spin around, my face awash with glee as I take in the sight of my best friend. Her long brown hair is tucked under a white hat with a fluffy pom pom on top, and her adorable red tipped nose tells me she's been out here for a hot minute. "I thought we were meeting you at the cabin."

"Surprise! I got in early and your last text said you were headed to the tree farm, so I did a little sleuthing and figured out where you'd be."

"Efficient and possibly a little creepy," I tease, wrapping my bestie in a crushing hug. As we pull apart, I notice the subtle shadows under her eyes. "How was the drive?"

"Peaceful." She sighs, and there's something in her tone that has me cocking my head in question. "Exams were exhausting," she explains, as if expecting an inquisition. She smiles, but it's not her usual bright, cheerful one. Maggie's my free-spirited bestie, but something's off and I can't quite place it. I tuck that thought away for later — now's not the time.

8

"Perfect timing," Cade interjects, a broad smile on his face. "You can help us pick a tree."

I lock elbows with one of my favorite people in the world, leaving my husband in the dust as we skip down the aisle, giggling along the way.

"How's Papa Watson?" I ask.

"Same as always. Way too wealthy for his own good, spends too much time pandering to the boys' club that is the board of directors at the magazine, and has a girlfriend way too many years his junior." With an eye roll, she tugs me towards a cluster of pine trees, obviously deflecting from the conversation at hand. Mags doesn't like to talk about her dad, but I know his lack of presence in her life hurts. The fact that he wants her to be his legacy when all she wants is her dad to be there for her must be difficult. I can clearly see the strain around her eyes, so I let the conversation float off into the ether, continuing our perusal of the various trees.

An hour later, we've got the 6ft pine tucked near the window in the den, wrapped in strands of warm white string lights. Several bags of brand new ornaments are strewn along the coffee table waiting to be placed on the tree, along with some antiques that I found while I was thrifting, but my energy is zapped. Pregnancy fatigue is a bitch.

"Here," Cade says, handing me the last stack of Nana's pizzelles and a peppermint tea for my nausea. "This should help. I need to run to the grocery store and grab some last-minute things for tomorrow." He turns to Mags next, handing her another cup of tea. "Take care of my girl, yeah?"

Maggie smiles, then quirks a brow. "Need I remind you she was my girl first?"

"Finders keepers," he teases.

"Before y'all start talking about the 5 second rule or some shit, I love you both, so shut the fuck up. I'm perfectly fine here, Cowboy. See you soon."

Cade shakes his head at my snark then kisses me sweetly before disappearing out the door, the faint chill from the cold air wafting into the space causing goosebumps to erupt along my arms. I pull Cade's hoodie a little tighter around myself and snag a blanket off the back of the couch for my legs.

My favorite Christmas candle is burning on the coffee table, permeating the room with the scent of vanilla and a hint of spice as the sound of my Christmas playlist filters through the speakers — I couldn't be more cozy and content.

"So tell me about this list," she says, holding up my scrap of paper with the holiday bucket on it. "Honestly, I think we can do better."

I gasp, feigning shock and indignation. "How dare you shit on my very detailed, very cutesy list!"

Maggie laughs at my theatrics, then procures a pen from her purse. "I'd be remiss if I didn't remind you of the great gingerbread house debacle of 2022. We need a redemption arc, babe."

"Are you sure that's a good idea? It looked like a crime scene the last time. Not unlike the pumpkin carving calamity of 2024."

"Pfft. We've got this," she says, adding it to the list. "I'll text Cade and let him know we need him to grab some stuff while he's out. Mags taps away at her phone and the group chat lights up with notifications.

> **Mags:** Bucket list emergency. We need stuff to make a gingerbread house.

> **Cade:** I think we need to have a chat about the definition of emergency, Mags.

> **Miles:** Should we really be trusting the muffin menace to bake cookies now, too?

> **Mags:** Shut it, Casper.

> Dean: They have kits for that now.

> Cara: The kits suck. They don't have nearly enough supplies and the gingerbread is always the flavor and texture of cardboard.

> Mags: Just do it, Cowboy.

> Cade: Send me a list. Better yet...

Seconds later, my phone vibrates with an incoming video chat. I tap accept and my gorgeous husband's rugged face fills the screen. "Hey Sunshine. I'm at the grocery store, here to fulfill your every gingerbread fantasy. Tell me what you need."

"Oh baby. I have so many gingerbread fantasies," I tease.

Mags slaps me on the arm. "Gross. Stop flirting and get to the good stuff."

"The flirting is the good stuff," Cade says with a quirk in his brow.

"Ok," I start. "We need three tubes of pre-made gingerbread dough from the cooler at the back. You following?"

"On it." The underside of Cade's jaw and the ceiling of the market are all I see as he pushes the cart to the back of the store. "Ok, dough secured. What's next?"

"Go to the baking aisle and grab the biggest bag of powdered sugar they have. Then go to the candy aisle." I continue to guide him around the store, instructing him to buy gumdrops, sprinkles, candy canes, and a plethora of other confections to adorn our gingerbread houses. Once I think we've got everything we need, we end the call, and I sink back into the comfort of my makeshift cocoon.

"He's a good egg," Mags says. "Didn't even question anything."

"He's the best," I agree through a yawn.

Mags slides off the sectional and snatches up a pack of

orange slice ornaments, tearing open the packaging. "Ok, babe. You point and I'll place."

"Oh, you don't have to do that. Just give me like 30 minutes and I'll be good as new." Even as the words come out, I know I'm minutes away from blissful slumber, but I don't want Mags to think she has to do this without me.

"Yeah, sure. If you want Cade to murder me, we can do that. Or, hear me out... you could just let people help you."

"Ugh, you're the worst."

"Love you, too."

As I watch Maggie decorating the tree, the stillness seeps into my bones, allowing me to fully relax for the first time in days, and before I know it I'm slipping off to sleep.

Mags

Unsurprisingly, it didn't take long for Paige to completely pass out on me, but I soldier on, anyway. She might be pissed that I finished without her, but as far as I'm concerned I'm team Cade on this one — she's working herself too hard. I'm just hanging the last teardrop ornament on the tree when Cade comes in, holding out a cocktail for me to take.

"Wow. This looks great," he says, gesturing to the tree with a nod of approval. It's covered in an eclectic mix of vintage ornaments, velvet bows, and wood beads. "How long has she been asleep?"

"About 30 minutes. She doing ok?"

"You know Paige," he scoffs. "Always trying to do it all."

"Some things never change." I hold up the list I found attached to the fridge as I sip the festive concoction. It tastes sweet with a hint of something spicy. "You really gonna go through with all this?"

He nods, looking over at his wife, who's shifted underneath the blanket. "Honestly, I think she needs the fun.

Between work and the pregnancy, she hasn't done anything for herself lately. I'm worried it's all going to catch up with her, eventually."

"Is that really why you're doing it? Or is it because you're so fucking in love you'd do anything to make her smile?" I ask with a knowing grin. He chuckles, letting me know I've hit the nail on the head.

Cade gives me a nod as Paige's sleepy voice interrupts our conversation. "You can stop talking about me like I'm not in the room." Cade and I exchange a look, bursting into unrestrained laughter.

"Assholes," she mutters.

"Good morning, sleepyhead," Cade says, taking a seat beside her on the plush sofa. He brushes a curl behind her ear to lay a soft kiss to her forehead, and the gesture sends a jolt of longing through my chest. They're disgustingly cute, and while I've never really thought about getting into anything long term (except maybe that one time), they make me want... more.

"It's been a long day. You good if I call it a night?" I ask, hesitating slightly. I want to spend time with my girl, but I'm teetering on the edge of complete exhaustion.

"Of course," Paige says, concern etched in the furrow of her brow as she scans my face. I give her a cheerful smile that even I know looks forced. "You remember where the guest room is?"

I nod before leaving the room, stopping to grab my bag near the door before climbing the stairs to the expansive second floor. The guest room is huge with a large king size bed, plush white linens, and a breathtaking view of the lake. If I hadn't already seen the primary bedroom, I would assume this was it.

Standing near the floor to ceiling windows, I gaze out at the scenery, exhaling a deep breath as I watch snowflakes dance

13

above the glassy surface. There's a peacefulness here that sets my soul at ease — it feels like I'm right where I need to be. For now, anyway. It never truly lasts.

Once I've showered and tucked myself into bed, my thoughts swirl over the fact that I'll be seeing Miles tomorrow at the party. I resolve to keep my distance and not let his presence and his antagonistic tendencies provoke me. I will not let some pompous asshole ruin my first Christmas in Oak Ridge. As far as I'm concerned, Miles Barlow can go fuck himself.

Chapter 3

Paige

♫ Wit it This Christmas - Ariana Grande

The morning is a chaotic hustle and bustle of party prep as I frantically put the finishing touches on our holiday decor. I'd make a mental note to start this shit earlier next year, but I know the thought will leave my chaotic brain as soon as I move on to the next task.

While I'm setting up the stepladder to attach some mistletoe to the archway between the kitchen and the den, I can feel a set of eyes boring holes in my skull. "Can I help you with something?" I ask, wiggling my ass suggestively.

"As much as I love the view, why don't you tell me why you need a stepladder and I'll climb up there for you," he says.

"I'm not helpless, babe."

"I didn't say you were, but sometimes you need to learn when to ask for help." He rakes a hand through his light brown hair, a little longer than he usually keeps it, but I like the extra length. He's ruggedly handsome — and all mine.

I let out a sigh of exasperation. "I'm trying to hang the

16

mistletoe," I say, holding the aforementioned decoration above my head with a quirk in my brow, tugging my bottom lip between my teeth.

Cade steps into my space, placing one massive hand on my waist as the other cups my jaw while his thumb pulls my lip free. Our eyes lock as he leans in for a slow, sensual kiss that leaves me breathless.

"Was that so hard?" he asks.

"Mmmm. Judging by the state of things — it was," I tease, glancing down at the noticeable bulge in his jeans. He groans, adjusting his erection.

"Sunshine..." There's a warning in his tone, one I have no intention of heading as I cup him over his jeans and nip at his chin. He groans, and before I can register what's happening, he's throwing me over his shoulder with a slap on my ass. He bounds up the stairs, setting me down in front of my wall to wall bookshelves in the library. "On your knees."

"Mmmmm. I love my bossy Cowboy," I say, sinking to the floor as Cade turns the lock on the door.

"Be a good girl and unbutton my jeans, baby." His deep voice is strained, much like his cock. I reach out and free it from its confines, looking up at Cade through my eyelashes. His jaw is clenched, his eyes full of lust. "Open," he commands, fisting my curly mass of hair and tugging just enough to tell me he's in control. Goosebumps erupt along my arms at the deep timber of his voice, and I become fully compliant, opening my mouth. Cade glides the head of his hard cock along my tongue, giving me a taste of his salty pre-cum. "That's my girl," he groans.

As I close my mouth around him, he holds me back. "You want my cock, baby?"

I nod as much as I can while he keeps me in place and his grip on my hair has me moaning around him. His gaze darkens as he pushes forward, hitting the back of my throat. I grip his thighs for purchase, allowing him to use me for his pleasure. "Touch yourself, my greedy girl. I want you to come while I stuff you full of my cock."

Pushing my hand under my leggings, I circle my clit with my fingers, feeling how wet I am just from sucking him off. Cade reaches down, pushing my off the shoulder sweater beneath my breasts, taking my bra with it. "So goddamn beautiful," he murmurs. With my free hand, I pinch my nipple while Cade continues to plunge all the way to the back of my throat. "Fuck. Your mouth is too good. I'm gonna cum."

I double my efforts, adding more pressure to my pussy while I suck the life out of Cade's cock. "Come with me, baby," he begs as he pulls out of my mouth, stroking himself, the muscles of his forearm rippling deliciously. The sight has my orgasm cresting. As he finishes on my chest, I crash over the edge, crying out my own release. Cade tucks himself back in his pants and helps me stand.

"I'll be right back," he says, kissing me on the forehead. Fixing my leggings, I sink down onto the plush settee when Cade returns with a wet washcloth. He cleans me up, then sets my clothing back into place. "Fucking hell, Sunshine. You're gonna be the death of me."

"Right back atcha, Cowboy. Now about that mistletoe..."

Chapter 4

Miles

♫ *Under the Mistletoe - Kelly Clarkson*

Maggie fucking Watson.

Ok, yeah. I knew she was going to be here. But did she have to show up looking like *that*? She's wearing some kind of low cut velvet dress with a slit that stops mid thigh, giving me a stunning view of her ASS-ets. From my spot at the kitchen island, I can just make out the top of her thigh highs. She's talking animatedly with Cara near the Christmas tree that looks like it was plucked straight out of a home decor magazine.

Honestly, the whole house is like a scene from a hallmark movie, with garland strung along the staircase, string lights around the windows, and led candles in antique brass holders scattered along every table and shelf. The embers crackle in the intricately decorated fireplace, enhancing the already cozy atmosphere. Even the bookshelves are lined with a collection of holiday classics, and vintage Christmas trinkets. It's a veritable wonderland, but all of it pales in comparison to the star of all my wet dreams.

"You're drooling," Cade says, nudging me with his elbow.

"Ahem. What?" When in doubt, pretend to be oblivious. It's worked well for me in the past. Everybody just assumes the blondes are completely clueless — I've learned to use it to my advantage.

"Sure. Keep pretending." Cade chuckles then walks into the den, wrapping his arms around Paige who melts into his arms. They're so in love it makes my stomach twist.

Relationships like theirs are one in a million and I'm happy for Cade. He deserves the best and Paige has given that to him in spades — I love her like a sister. Unfortunately for me, she comes as a package deal wrapped up in a neat little Maggie shaped bow. And that particular Christmas vixen would rather shit in her hands and clap than be within eyeshot of me, so I'm keeping my distance. That is until Paige announces it's time for the secret Santa gift exchange. *Great.*

In our running group text, Paige laid out the rules for the exchange, then directed us to use an app to find our pairings. We had a $20 budget and the goal was to pick the funniest gift. I was grateful when the app paired me with Liam. Was I a little nervous I'd end up with Maggie? Hell yeah, I was. I was 100% prepared to fake an illness, or jump in front of oncoming traffic.

"Ok, everybody take a piece of paper from a hat so we can determine who picks first. And a friendly reminder, you're not supposed to know who you were paired with, so keep your big mouths shut until everyone has opened their gifts." Paige's eyes narrow on me and I wink, mouthing a "who me?" with an innocent smile. She just shakes her head and continues handing out slips of paper.

Cara's the first to go, snatching a small red gift bag under the tree. She pulls out a gardening t-shirt that says "Hoeing ain't easy" and she immediately scans the room looking for the culprit. Nobody gives anything away and we carry on. If nothing else, this game is going to be an education. I had no idea Cara was into gardening. The more you know, I guess.

Up next is Dean. His package is meticulously wrapped, so I assume he was paired with one of the women. He tears open the green paper to find a pair of boxers that say "This cock belongs to Cara" in big bold writing with a Rooster in the middle. I snort into my glass of whiskey, and Mags rolls her eyes at me from across the room.

Paige takes the next turn, snagging a medium sized gift bag with mismatched tissue paper. Inside is a white frilly apron with a huge muffin on the front that says "Muffin Menace" in large purple bubble letters.

Cade goes next, pulling out a hoodie. On it, there's a cartoon cat that looks suspiciously like Goose dressed as a cowboy, with the words "you've buttered your last biscuit" underneath the quirky feline portrait. "Don't you even think about stealing this one," he says, his eyes trained on his wife as she sticks out her tongue in his direction.

Assessing the context clues thus far, I would assume the couples were suspiciously paired with each other. Up next is Liam, and I take a drink to hide my smirk. He chuckles as he unwraps a pair of custom socks with my face all over them, eliciting several snorts from around the room.

"Miles... the point of the game was that nobody would know who bought the gifts, you absolute fruitcake," Paige chastises with a playful smack on my chest. I just shrug, catching Maggie's stare from across the room. There's a slight tilt to her lips and it feels like a win. She quickly glances away, taking another drink of her cocktail, washing away any sign that the expression was ever there, but it's too late — I made Maggie Watson smile.

"Holy shit. Have y'all looked outside lately?" Ivy asks from her spot on the floor near the window. "It's a complete white out."

Several of us scramble to our feet, taking in the view from the floor to ceiling windows. She wasn't kidding. The sky is absolutely dumping snow on us and the roads are likely to be a mess within the hour. "Should we call it a night?" Paige asks, her tone filled with disappointment as she peers out at the scene. Our cars are already covered in a blanket of fresh powder, and it's not letting up

"Or, we could turn this into a slumber party," Cara suggests. "Let's be realistic — several of you are already on your way to being drunk — I'm looking at you Mags — and it would be safer if we just hunker down. If that's alright with y'all?"

"The kids are already asleep upstairs so it's probably best if we stick around," Ivy adds.

Cade looks to Paige for approval. She nods and the decision is made.

"It's so beautiful," Paige says with a smile lighting up her face. "Think it'll stick around for Christmas?"

"I wouldn't count on it. Kentucky's not known for having white Christmases very often," I explain.

Paige's posture deflates and Maggie chimes in. "Shut up, Miles. It's still possible." I hold up my hands in a gesture of surrender and we return to the game.

The little Christmas vixen is next. Maggie giggles and kicks her feets as she opens a bag of phallic gummies. She stumbles over the words as she reads the label aloud for everyone — "Eat a bag of dicks." Her nose is adorably scrunched and I want to kiss it. *Shit, where did that thought come from?* I don't do tenderness. I fuck fast and hard, then get the hell out of there. Don't get me wrong — I make sure everyone is satisfied. More than once. But I don't have the capacity for anything beyond that.

Next, Ivy opens a small envelope with a very detailed train ticket that says the final destination is 'Pound Town' — that one gets the most laughs. She clutches the ticket to her chest dramatically, "Oh, Santa! How did you know? It's been so long since I've made the trip home." Paige is nearly doubled over laughing at this point — it doesn't take much to get her going.

Once the laughter subsides, I down my drink. There's one gift left under the tree, and it's mine. Unfortunately for me, I think I know exactly who it's from as she watches me attentively from across the room, trying to hide her smile behind the nearly empty cocktail glass. I hesitantly approach the tree, picking up a rectangular package. Tearing open the reindeer wrapping paper, I pull out a VHS copy of the 90's classic, Ghost. The joke sails over everyone else's heads as I stare daggers at my nemesis, who's sporting a sexy smirk. And, fuck — why it *that* so goddamn hot.

I can't even hate her for this; it was a brilliant move in the grand scheme of things — check and mate. Fuck my life. This girl is going to be the death of me.

Our complicated history has our friends exchanging questioning glances. Nobody knows what really went down between Mags and I — and they never will. Maggie doesn't even have the full story.

Cade gives me an assessing stare, then diverts the attention away from me. "Ok, so I think most of the pairings were pretty obvious, but who gave Mags a bag of dicks?"

Liam chuckles, "That would be me. Who gave Ivy the ticket to pound town?"

"Guilty," Cara says.

"Wait, so that means the cock underwear was actually Ivy? I really thought it was Cara staking her claim." Paige snorts.

"Nope, but I appreciate the assist," Cara jokes, giving Ivy a high five.

Snatching up the VHS, I head back into the kitchen to top off my drink.

"You good, man?" *Of course Cade would notice something is off.*

"Great," I deadpan. "Just grabbing another drink." I say, lifting the high ball up in salute before downing two fingers of Kentucky bourbon in one gulp.

"Look —" he starts, but he's cut off when Paige runs past us into the bathroom. "This isn't over. We'll talk later." Grateful for the reprieve, I pour another one and throw back a shot of tequila for good measure.

With my refill in hand, I stride back to the den, slamming into Maggie on the threshold.

"Miles." My name on her lips has my cock hardening. *Down boy.*

"If you'll just excuse me —" I start, but Maggie stops me with a hand on my chest, her gaze flicking overhead. Her intoxicating scent surrounds me as her fingertips gently glide down my torso. Fucking mistletoe.

"We shouldn't," I say, but my voice holds little conviction. I want nothing more than to claim her right here and right now.

"It's bad luck if we don't," she murmurs.

If I know anything about Maggie Watson, it's that she's not one to tempt fate or fuck around with superstitions. "In that case," I say, cupping her cheek in my palm. I know this is a terrible idea. Maybe it's the whiskey pulsing through my veins, or the fact that I've dreamt of Maggie's lips for months, if not longer, but I can't bring myself to stop what happens next. I stare into her golden irises, searching for any sign of trepidation finding only sweltering heat. She's fucking gorgeous and no way in hell am I passing up this opportunity.

"What are you waiting f —" Her words are cut off by a mischievous orange cat who takes that moment to dig his claws into my jeans, sending a sharp pain up my calf. I curse on impact, startling Mags.

"Shit. This was a mistake," she says, pushing against my chest before darting out of the room, leaving me rock hard and confused as hell. *What the fuck just happened?*

"Fucking cockblock." I pick up the demon cat who settles against my chest with a contented purr.

Chapter 5

Paige

♫ *Let It Snow - Tori Kelly & Babyface*

I lean over the kitchen island, checking 'Secret Santa' off the list, as my best friend hunches over her bowl of cereal, sighing dramatically.

"What's got you looking like someone kicked your cat?" I ask. She continues to push her soggy cereal around the bowl, absentmindedly dunking the star-shaped marshmallows, completely ignoring my question. "Mags?"

Her eyes snap up to meet my questioning stare. "What? Sorry, didn't hear you."

"Yeah, I got that. What's going on with you?"

"Oh, nothing. Just hungover." Her voice is full of fake brightness. I nod, not believing a single word. But as soon as I start to pry, I know she'll close herself off. Mags is an open book about most things, but she'll lock herself down like Fort Knox if you try to dig too deep. "How are you feeling?"

The abrupt subject change isn't a shock, and I let her get

away with it — for now. "I'm good. Who knew morning sickness was like an all day thing?"

"Pretty much everyone who's ever had a baby," she snorts, a little of the Mags I know bubbling to the surface, but it's gone as soon as Miles walks into the room, snagging the coffeepot from the counter. Her cheerful smile is quickly replaced by a mask of indifference.

"So it looks like we're gonna be stuck here for a while," he says, swiping on the local news app on his phone. "The roads are a mess. Cars in the ditch on every county road."

"Guess we'll hunker down," Cade says, walking into the room with a smirk meant only for me. I clench my thighs together, remembering our bedtime activities from the night before, his gruff voice commanding me to stay quiet as his cock plunged deep into my —

"Earth to Paige," Ivy says. I don't even know when she joined our merry band of misfits, and I have no idea what they've been talking about as I was lost in my own personal porn highlight reel. Cade smiles into his coffee, stifling a laugh before winking at me.

"Ugh," she grumbles. "Get a room. Some of us aren't getting any, and you're making it so much worse," she says.

"Might I suggest a magic wand and a book boyfriend?" I say, quirking a brow.

"Mommy! I want magic!" Rylin says, her bouncing curls barely visible above the countertop as she attempts to climb onto a stool. The entire room erupts into snorts and laughter, Cade nearly spitting his coffee clear across the room as Mags reaches down to help her up.

"Ooook, so what do we want to do today?" I ask, trying to steer the conversion into a more child friendly direction. I'm going to have to work on having a filter over the next few months or this baby is going to get an earful.

"We could work on your list," Cade suggests. "I picked up

those sleds from Archie yesterday and a few extra sets of winter gear just in case, so we should be good to go."

I glance over his shoulder as Miles swipes through the forecast on his phone again, and I wonder why he hasn't looked up once since he walked into the room. "Hell yeah! Suns out. We're getting another dusting later, but it looks like a decent day for it."

Scanning the group, I search for any signs of protest, but it seems like everyone is on board, so we finish our breakfasts and head off to our rooms. Last night, Liam and Miles each took a side of the oversized sectional, while Mags and Ivy shared the biggest guest bed. Dean and Cara set up an air mattress in the unfinished nursery, and the kids were already safely tucked away in the library before the storm hit.

Nobody came prepared for a multi-day event, but we scrounged up enough winter gear, or layer up some sweats to keep everyone warm. I make a mental note to do a load of everyone's laundry, so we're prepared in the likely event that they need to stay another night.

Once we're all standing by the door in several layers of clothing, I pass around a bin full of hats, scarves, and gloves. Miles is the last to pick, and he ends up with a bright pink beanie with a pompom on top. He tugs it over his blonde hair with zero hesitation, eliciting a huff of laughter from Mags as she reads the embroidery on the front: Fuck the Patriarchy. Her face drops as realization dawns, no doubt recalling the day she gifted it to me.

Mags

I almost kissed Miles fucking Barlow.

And now that fucker is wearing my hat. Ok, not mine, but I bought it for Paige. Last night, I went to bed wet and needy. I couldn't even do anything about it with Ivy at my side.

Besides, I wasn't about to get myself off to thoughts of the man who... nevermind. It's ancient history and I'm not going to give it anymore of my energy. Good vibes only, Mags.

Paige leads the cavalry out to the backyard. The once brown, dreary landscape has been replaced by a winter wonderland overnight, another fine sprinkling of flakes slowly fluttering to the ground. A delicate snowflake lands on the tip of my nose, and a thumb reaches out to brush it off. Miles.

I glare up at the interloper, putting a good 3 feet of space between us. I don't know why he's constantly in my orbit, but I have got to keep my distance so I don't murder him — or worse, kiss him. "What's wrong, Wildcat?" he asks, a glint of amusement in his eyes. I flash him a middle finger, though it's somewhat stifled by the fuzzy yellow mittens, and he chuckles.

Yep. Homicide. Definitely homicide.

"Ok boys," Paige says, rounding up her troops like a drill sergeant. "I need you to go down the hill and make a barrier. The last thing we need is someone plowing straight into the lake. "Girls, we're going to sit back and ogle the eye candy."

"Candy?" Rylin's eyes light up with excitement at the mention of sweet treats.

"Not that kind of candy, sweetie." Paige says, giving her a boop on the nose. Rylin's body deflates with disappointment. "But once we go inside later, we'll have hot chocolate!" That perks her right back up, and I can't help the swell of affection for this sweet little girl. I've never wanted kids for myself — I'm a wanderer at heart. But I love being Auntie Mags. I get to spoil them rotten, then give them right back to their parents — best of both worlds.

All of us girls settle on the back steps, watching the muscle do their thing without a single protest. Paige has an entire boy band at her beck and call — love that for her.

"Damn, Paige. This could be a why choose situation," Ivy teases. "Remind me again why you're not more of a slut?"

"Hey now, one of those hotties is mine." Cara playfully smacks Ivy across the arm. "And I don't share."

"Still, that leaves two more unclaimed," Ivy notes.

A pang of something I can't quite place spears my chest at the thought of Miles with anyone else, but I don't have time to unpack all of that. I shake it off, resolved to ignore him for the rest of this gods forsaken trip.

Ivy

You could cut the Miles and Mags tension with a butter knife, and I didn't miss the look on her face when I suggested Paige take a ride on that particular train to Pound Town.

Aidan and Rylin are building a tiny snowman at the foot of the stairs and it sends a jolt of longing through my chest. I've always wanted Ry to have a sibling, but with my shitty husband out of the picture combined with the promise I made to myself to never get tied up with love again, it looks like that desire is dead on arrival. Aidan is already like a big brother to Ry, so I'm grateful she'll at least have him in her life. He helps her smooth out the head of her snowman and she looks up at him like he hung the moon. I wish someone would look at me that way.

"Done," Cade calls from the bottom of the hill, pointing to a newly erected snow barrier. It looks formidable, but there's only one way to find out. Without a second thought, I snag the saucer sled off the porch and throw myself down the hill at breakneck speed. Sounds of laughter and joy ring out as I giggle all the way down the hill, coming to a stop just short of the wall.

Miles reaches out a hand to help me up with an impressed expression. "Damn, Ivy. Didn't know you had it in you."

"What? Happiness?" I snort.

"I was thinking more like a rebellious streak. How was it?"

"Like being a kid again," I reply. I'm smiling from ear to ear until my thoughts spiral back to my childhood, stopping me in my tracks. Before I can let myself get too deep into that black hole, a giggling Rylin comes down the hill with Paige behind her on a wooden sled. My girl is practically beaming when they reach the bottom.

She squeals, "Again! Again!"

Tugging on her hands to help her to stand, I dust off her snow covered legs. "Let's give some other people a turn and then we'll go together, ok?"

"Otay, Mommy," she says in her sweet little 3-year-old voice. She started preschool a few months ago, and her vocabulary has drastically improved save for a few hard c and k words. Truthfully, I'm not ready for her to drop that little quirk. I just want to keep her little for as long as possible.

The entire group trudges back up the hill just in time to see Aidan settling on the magic carpet, an infectious smile spread across his cheeks. Mags gives him a soft push, and we watch him slide down the hill with a look of childlike wonder on his face as he glances back at his dad for approval. Liam stands with his arms grossed, his usually grumpy facade momentarily cracking as he gives his son a thumbs up.

"Yay Aidan!" Rylin cheers. Liam and I exchange smiles; I don't know much about his history except that his ex left Aidan on his doorstep a little more than a year ago, thrusting an unprepared Liam straight into fatherhood. He's a great dad, but I think he has a tendency to doubt himself. He works hard for his kid and it shows. I wish I could've given that kind of father figure to Rylin, but I'm stuck filling in for a piece of shit who only uses her to keep up appearances with his family and the public.

Barely a foot away, Mags lowers herself onto the saucer, but she's stuck rooted to the spot as she tries to propel herself forward. "Little help?" she asks, glancing around at the crew for assistance. I start to move but to no one's surprise, Miles steps forward first, kneeling behind her.

"Gods. Anybody but you," she mutters under her breath, just loud enough for Liam and I to catch it, giving each other a knowing look. He leans over and whispers something in her ear, but this time it's too quiet to make out. Her body goes rigid just before he gives her a push, sending her barreling down the hill. She squeals on the way down, the anger instantly evaporating as she spins around, ending the slide completely backwards. Mags reaches the bottom with a whoop, throwing her fist in the air as she strikes a pose.

Mags helps Aidan back up the hill as Cade steps up to the mouth of the now well-worn path we've carved out. "Ready?" Cade asks, gesturing for Paige to join him on the wooden sled she calls the toboggan, though there's some debate over that title. She scoots to the front as Cade wraps himself around her, no doubt out of concern for both his wife and his daughter. A silent understanding passes between them as Paige grips the rope.

"Someone give us a push?" he asks.

Liam crouches down and places his hands on Cade's back, giving them a gentle shove before joining me at the base of the stairs.

Time seems to slow as they race down the hill, gliding effortlessly at first. But then, just as they reach the bottom, they hit a patch of ice, sending them careening through the makeshift barrier to shocked gasps and howls of concern.

"Cade!" I shout.

At the last second, he jerks the sled to the left, instinctively pushing Paige over the side, a flash of fear in her eyes as she tumbles into the powdery, untouched snow. I watch in horror as Cade rolls onto the barely frozen surface of the lake, the ice cracking ominously beneath him.

Miles takes off down the hill, his expression shifting from amusement to abject horror, Mags following hot on his heels.

"Fuck!" Liam curses. "There's no fucking way the ice will hold for long." In a flash, he's barrelling down the hill after them. Cade grapples for purchase, trying to pull himself back onto solid ground as the ice cracks underneath him.

I want to move, to do something — anything at all — but I'm frozen, fear keeping me rooted in place. Miles reaches out for Cade, desperation in his eyes. "Take my hand!" he shouts.

Cade grasps Miles's hand while Liam grabs his other, and they work together to haul him back onto shore. A collective sigh of relief escapes the group, but it's tinged with lingering worry.

Paige, now on her feet, rushes to Cade, tears streaming down her cheeks. "I'm so sorry! This was a terrible idea," she cries, her voice choked with emotion. Cade pulls her close, one hand cradling her face while the other lands on her bump as he murmurs soothing words nobody else can hear.

"Let's get everyone inside," I say, more to myself than anyone else, my voice shaking slightly. I turn to the kids, who have been blissfully unaware of the chaos, and gently guide them inside, to their utter disappointment.

Once I have them set up in the living room with a movie, I head back outside to check on my friends. The tension hangs heavy in the air as I find the group gathered at the top of the hill, looking haggard yet relieved.

"Are you okay?" I ask. Cade nods, though his expression betrays the adrenaline still coursing through him.

"Fuck, that was terrifying," he admits, pulling Paige close. She looks up at him, still teary-eyed but visibly calming.

"It's all my fault," she whispers.

"Hey," he murmurs. Pulling her into his chest, he kisses her forehead. "Accidents happen, baby. It's not your fault. I'm okay. We're okay." They stand there holding each other, and I feel like an intruder in their private moment, so I take several steps back, giving them some space.

Cade's quiet reassurances seem to calm her enough to head inside. Warmth envelopes us as we step into the cabin. With a reassuring nod, Paige and Cade immediately disappear upstairs.

After removing all of my wet outerwear, I head into the den, settling Rylin on my lap with a fluffy blanket.

"Dad, can I have hot cocoa now?" Aidan asks as Liam walks into the room.

"Sure, bud. Come on." He takes his son by the hand and disappears into the kitchen, leaving me alone in the silence with an exhausted toddler and my spiraling thoughts. What I wouldn't give to have a love like Paige and Cade. Where they love out loud and face every challenge as a team.

It's not long before Rylin falls asleep with her head on my chest, her quiet snores breaking through the quiet. She'll be pissed if she misses out on hot chocolate, so I make a mental note to ask Paige if she can keep the crock pot on for when she wakes up.

I stroke a hand over Rylin's curls. She smells a little like a wet dog but I'm too exhausted to bring her upstairs. My eyes grow heavy and it's not long before I'm drifting off to sleep alongside her.

Chapter 6

Cara

♫ *A Nonsense Christmas - Sabrina Carpenter*

After the excitement of the day, I just want to stand under a stream of hot water and bring the feeling back to my extremities. Cade and Paige disappeared into their room, returning looking refreshed and no worse for the wear. I'll never forget the terror as we watched them break through the barrier. I'm just grateful it wasn't much worse.

"You good, Daze?" *Daze. Ugh, that nickname goes straight to my pussy every time.*

Dean and I met briefly on the last day of highschool while I was plucking petals off a daisy. Completely unbeknownst to him, Dean had been the star of all my fantasies, and the subject of my "he loves me, he loves me not" for much of my high school career. Nothing ever came of it; I was always the fat girl with red hair who didn't quite fit in. I've outgrown the person I was in my teens, and while I'm still fat, and I still have my signature long ginger locks, I no longer give a fuck what anybody else thinks of me.

Years later, every single one of my fantasies has come true. Ok, maybe not all of them. I'm still Cara Kirkpatrick — for now. If only 16-year-old me knew where life would take her just 10 years later — wrapped up in the arms of the only person I ever truly wanted, hoping one day he'd be down on one knee, sliding a ring on my finger. Maybe I should take a page out of Paige's playbook and do the asking myself. I'm a confident woman, but I'm not sure if I'm that confident. And there's something to be said for letting the man I love sweep me off my feet.

"Hey," Dean whispers, brushing a lock of hair off my forehead. "Where'd you go?"

"Just thinkin'," I say with a smile.

His brow furrows. "About?"

"You." Immediately, his gaze turns heated, and he shifts on the spot.

"Daze, if you want me to fuck you, all you have to do is ask."

I slap him on the chest. "Shhh. We're literally surrounded by our friends."

"And they can hear you," Miles chuckles.

"Got a really great shower upstairs," Cade remarks with a quirk in his brow. That's all Dean needs to hear as he throws me over his shoulder and carries me up the stairs, leaving a chorus of laughter and cheers behind.

"Put me down, you menace. I'm not fucking you in your best friend's house while they're all downstairs listening."

He places me back on my feet near the massive walk-in shower. It's all sleek and pristine, with sage green tiles and gold fixtures. "Do you really think Paige and Cade haven't had sex since we got here? I'm pretty sure he just railed her six ways from Sunday after that near death experience."

"But — "He cuts me off with a punishing kiss, his tongue dancing along the seam of my lips, begging for entry. His familiar woody scent surrounds me as our bodies collide, and every bit of reluctance disappears right alongside any thought of our friends one floor away.

"Fuck, Daze. I'll never get enough of you." His hands find the hem of my hoodie, tugging it over my head along with the t-shirt and sweatpants, leaving me bare except for my matching red lace bra and panties. Dean's gaze darkens as he steps back to pull his own shirt off, giving me a mouthwatering view of every ripple and ridge of his toned torso. His messy, dark brown hair falls over his forehead as his chocolate irises spear me with need. He's every single one of my fantasies come true. I'll admit to being a little self-conscious the first time we had sex. But Dean instinctively knew exactly what I needed, whispering beautiful words as he worshiped every single dip and curve of my size 24 body.

I can't help but run my palms over my breasts, moaning as I watch my man remove every stitch of his clothing, freeing his beautiful, hard cock — yes, I said beautiful. It's a heady feeling, knowing that this man belongs to me.

He stalks towards me like a man on a mission. "You wet for me, love?"

"Yes," I say on a sigh. His hands skate around to my ass, pulling me into him as his length pushes into my soft belly. Dean's 6'3" frame cages me against the wall as he lays agonizingly slow kisses along my collarbone. My hands fist in mussed up golden brown hair, guiding his mouth to where I ache for him. Dean takes one peeked nipple between his lips and tugs, eliciting a strangled moan from deep in my chest.

Whether the goosebumps along my skin are from his sinful mouth or the remnants of our time spent in the snow, I'll never know. "We should get in the shower." My voice is breathy, and I can feel the wetness pooling between my thighs at every brush of his lips on my silken skin.

"Feeling needy? Gonna let me come in your pretty pussy?"

"God yes."

Dean intertwines our fingers in a tender gesture before tugging me towards the shower. One arm wraps around my waist stroking soothing circles along my skin like he can't stand to not be touching me at all times. With the other hand, he adjusts the knobs and tests the water until steam begins to fog up the glass. Once inside, his reverent touches turn hungry again. My stomach does a little flip when he pulls down the retractable shower head and sets it to the highest setting.

His hand trails down my stomach to my core, already soaked and needy.

"Need to watch you come for me, Daze." He whispers, before replacing his hand with the showerhead.

"Oh god," I moan. "Feels so good." His mouth finds my nipple and tugs, causing my pussy to clench around nothing, and I immediately feel empty. "More," I plead.

"Tell me what you need, love."

"You."

"My fingers?" he asks, plunging 2 of his thick fingers into my pussy

"No. Need your cock."

"Mmmm..." His groan vibrates through his chest into mine as I throw my head back against the tile. "Gonna need you to come for me first."

"Please."

"Such a needy girl," he chuckles darkly as his fingers curl and find the spot that's guaranteed to make me unravel.

"Fuck." My eyes squeeze shut as I try to concentrate on his fingers. Dean knows it takes a little extra work to get me there as my mind often becomes unfocused and erratic, so he starts to whisper filthy words in my ear, coaxing my orgasm.

"Come on my fingers, Daze. Wanna watch you fall apart and drip all over my hand. Then I'm gonna fuck you rough and deep until you come on my cock. I won't stop until you're begging me to fill you up." Breeding kink engaged.

"Oh shit, I'm so close." Dean angles the stream a little closer to my clit and I detonate; the only thing keeping me on my feet is Dean's strong arm holding me against the wall.

"So fucking pretty when you come apart for me." He carefully replaces the showerhead on its perch and returns to me, my body still coming down from the high of my first orgasm. I have no doubt he'll make good on every filthy promise.

Dean

I'm so fucking in love with her. My gorgeous girl. My Daisy. I spin her away from me, pushing her up against the tile.

"God, yes!" she moans. She's already wet from her first orgasm as I glide my length over her clit and back down, reveling in the silky smoothe feel of her pussy as I tease her relentlessly until she's writhing beneath me.

"You're gonna take all of me, aren't you, love? Gonna let me fill this pretty pussy and watch you come all over my cock." Lining myself up where I know she's aching for me, I push forward in one gentle stroke, easing my way in before I pull back out again.

"Please," she begs. "I need more."

Her words unravel me and I plunge forward, her body giving no resistance. I thrust my hips at a punishing pace, bottoming out over and over as she moans and meets me thrust for thrust. Her round ass bounces with each movement and it's the most erotic sight.

"Fuck, Daze. This body. What you do to me. I'll never get enough of you."

"Make me come, Dean." Her breaths are coming in pants now; her red hair falling down her back as I thread my fingers through the wet tresses, pulling her head to the side to expose her neck. My lips find her collarbone, feeling the goosebumps erupting along her flesh. My other hand snakes around her body, finding her swollen clit as her pussy clenches.

"I'm gonna come," she pants. "Fuck."

"I'm right behind you, Daze. Let go, love."

I continue stroking her in smooth circles, keeping a steady pace just the way she likes it. In two more rough thrusts, she falls apart, her nails digging into my forearm to keep herself upright. The pulsing from her orgasm pulls me over the edge with her, our bodies spent as the steam from the shower surrounds us.

I spin her around, bringing her mouth to mine in a languid kiss. "Give me one more," I say, sinking to my knees to worship at her feet — right where I belong.

Three orgasms later, I wrap my girl in a fluffy robe and we head down the hall to dress. If I'm being honest, I was more than happy to be snowed in — it gave me a much needed reprieve from the daily monotony of work. And obviously I'm not going to turn down quality time with Cara.

She works her ass off at the hospital, crawling into my bed completely exhausted most nights. Despite the fact that she spends damn near every night in my bed, she still hasn't officially moved in with me. But I'll make it happen one way or another. Soon.

Once dressed, we head back into the kitchen, feeling warm and refreshed. Miles smirks from his spot at the island, taking a long sip of hot cocoa from a novelty snowman mug.

"Hey there, Daze," he says, holding up the mug in a mock salute.

With a glare, I slap Miles upside the head for goading me. "Fuck off, dipshit."

Cara laughs, sliding her hand down my spine as she walks over to the crock pot. "Pleeeease tell me you didn't finish all the hot cocoa."

"Nope, plenty left," he says, before leaving us alone in the kitchen. I walk over to Cara, wrapping my arms around her waist, kissing the spot behind her ear that never fails to make her melt. "Love you," I whisper. She smells like her coconut lotion. So familiar — like home.

"If you want some hot cocoa, all you have to do is ask." She giggles and I tickle her ribs in retaliation, then snag the Santa mug right out of her hand. "Hey! Rude!" she says, tossing a giant marshmallow at my head. I duck and it soars straight past me, hitting a scowling Liam in the face as Aidan bursts into a fit of laughter.

Cara's expression turns sheepish as she eyes Liam, but a smile breaks out across his face, easing the tension. "I'll get you for that later," he teases, pointing 2 fingers to his eyes and back at Cara.

"Bright it on."

Chapter 7

Liam

♫ *Merry Christmas - Ed Sheeran and Elton John*

As much as I love my friends, I'm fucking wiped. The closer we get to Christmas, the worse my workload gets. Statistically speaking, the holidays bring about more fires, which means more call outs at the station. And The Ridge has been packed all week with depressed, lonely people trying to drink away their past, or forget that they have no one to share the holidays with.

Can't say I blame 'em. Hell, after Breanna left, I was one of 'em. But I have Aidan now and I can't remember my life before he existed. Working two jobs on top of being a single dad keeps me busy, so I'm grateful for the snow, if only for the break. I've thought about giving up my bartending gig at The Ridge, but I can't bring myself to leave Cade high and dry when he just took over ownership. That's a thought for further down the road.

Balancing work at the bar and the fire station along with

being a dad has been a challenge, but Aidan's thriving and that's good enough for me. I haven't always been the best man, but as soon as that 5-year-old boy showed up on my doorstep, I swore I'd never abandon him the way his mother did. And I would never become a piece of shit like my father. Growing up in the system because your parents are deadbeats isn't something I would wish on any child, much less my own.

"How's the forecast lookin'?" Miles asks, snapping me out of my dark thoughts. I'd been staring at the radar, unblinking, for god knows how long.

"Looks like another round late tonight. We might be stuck here for a while longer. Heard they've got the Hayes brothers out delivering groceries on their ATVs."

Cade sits down on the other end of the sectional, cradling a sleeping cat. Never thought Cade Brooks would be a cat dad. "Y'all are welcome to stay as long as you need. But I can't promise my wife won't put you to work."

I chuckle, recalling Paige sobbing into her poutine earlier this week because the cheese wasn't squeaky enough — whatever that means.

"You talking shit about me, Cowboy?" Paige saunters into the room with Aiden at her side, the scent of something delicious wafting through the room.

"Dad! Auntie Paige made chocolate muffins, and she said we could help her make —" he turns to Paige with a contemplative look on his face. "What did you say we were making?"

Paige laughs and ruffles his curly red hair. "They're called pizzelles, bud. They're cookies that look a little bit like snowflakes."

"Yeah! Can we dad?" His eyes are full of hope and anticipation, and there's no way in hell I'll be able to say no to that if Paige has already offered. I can't help but think that this is something he should be doing with his mom this time of year

— but she's off living her life as though he never existed, and I don't know the first thing about baking.

"Sure, buddy. As long as Auntie Paige says it's okay. And you have to listen to everything she says. Got it?"

Aidan pumps his fist in the air with a loud "Yes!" and a smile tugs at my lips. We've come a long way in the last 2 years; some days are harder than others. Being left on a stranger's doorstep at 5 years old comes with a lot of unresolved trauma. All things considered, he's made a lot of progress since arriving in Oak Ridge and he's the sweetest kid, in spite of everything he's been through. Why his mother left him with a grumpy asshole like me and not her parents is beyond me, but I'm glad she did. It's probably the only thing she ever did right by him. Or me, for that matter.

"You're not off the hook either, Broody McBartender," she says.

Miles snorts into what has to be his 4th or fifth round of hot cocoa; I suspect he's spiked it with something. Actually — that's not a bad idea. As I'm leaning in to ask Miles where he's keeping the Bailey's, Paige cuts me off. "Listen up! We're all pitching in for pizzelles this year. I plan to deliver them around town once the streets are open again, so that means it's all hands on deck."

I grumble under my breath, but clearly I wasn't quiet enough because Paige glares at me and Cade snakes an arm around her waist to keep her from lunging. Pregnant Paige is scary on a good day. She's either feral and protective, or a snotty sobbing mess. I'd say I feel sorry for Cade, but I've never seen him happier, and honestly, we all love her. Nobody else could get away with that ridiculous name but Paige. And maybe... nevermind.

An hour later, we're all set up in the kitchen with baking ingredients lining the island, and our marching orders. The kids are seated at the breakfast nook with stacking instructions and Ivy as a supervisor. Paige and Mags each have what looks like a waffle iron, and all the guys are sitting on the opposite side, with Christmas cards, a list of names, and gift wrapping supplies. As the large stand mixer stirs the first batch of batter, the air fills with the scent of black licorice and sugar. Miles casually slides a mug of hot cocoa across the island with a wink, then passes another to Cade. Thank fuck. I'll need more than a little liquor to get through this.

What feels like 800 pizzelles and 5 mugs of Miles' spiked cocoa later, my fingers are tingling, and there's a buzz thrumming in my veins. As I'm bagging another haphazardly wrapped stack of pizzelles, my phone chimes with a text notification.

> Goldie: Snowed in. Heard Connor sold the bar?

Fucking hell.

Paige

The warm feeling of contentment settles over me as the scent of pizzelles lingers in the air. These last couple of days have been a dream — spending the holidays with my chosen family. I can't remember the last time I felt so... settled. I'm just setting up a movie night in the den when all of the lights go out, plunging us into darkness.

"Looks like that second round of snow is on its way," Cade says. "I'll grab the candles and start a fire. You sit down before you hurt yourself, Sunshine."

Rolling my eyes, I feel my way around the room and sink

down into the cushions, wincing as my hip accidentally hits the stiff arm of the sofa. "Fuck."

"You good, babe?" A voice that's unmistakably Mags asks from somewhere to my left.

"All good," I reply. As my eyes adjust to the darkness, I see the vague outline of three figures seated on the sofa. Mags, Ivy, and Rylin.

"Mommy, I scared," Rylin sniffles.

"It's okay, Ryry. Uncle Cade is getting us some candles so we'll be able to see real soon, ok?" In the meantime, I pull out my phone and turn on the flashlight, placing it face down on the coffee table.

"Otay," she says, crawling over Mags to settle herself on my lap.

"Well, fuck me, I guess," Ivy says with a snicker.

Cade returns with a box full of our leftover LED candles from the wedding and places them around the room, creating an almost magical atmosphere. As he neatly stacks more logs in the fireplace, I unabashedly watch every muscle of his forearms flexing beneath his rolled up henley. I practically pant as he dips down, giving me an unobstructed view of his round ass as he lights the kindling.

Once the fire is crackling, enveloping the room in its warm glow, he turns around and catches me in the act, sending a wink in my direction.

"Whatdaya say we read some stories?" I ask, Ry's face lighting up with excitement as she nods vigorously, clapping her hands.

I send Cade upstairs to my library, where I keep a stash of books for when our little one arrives. He comes back with a vintage copy of The Night Before Christmas, the rest of our friends in tow as they settle around the room for our movie night turned story time. With any luck, the kiddos will fall asleep and the adults can have some fun of our own later.

Cade sinks down beside me as Rylin tucks herself into his side and sighs. He curls an arm around her shoulder and opens the book for her to follow along.

"Aidan, there's a spot for you over here too, if you want to see." He doesn't waste a second before sinking down on Cade's other side and my heart melts at the sight of my husband and the two sweetest kids in the world. He's going to be an incredible dad.

As he begins reading, the deep timbre of his voice reverberates through the silent room, sending a shiver up my spine and a rush of heat through my body. His voice still affects me, as it did during our very first phone call. Sometimes I wonder if I should ask him to sing a Josh Turner song as foreplay; I'm 100% certain it could get me halfway to orgasm before he even touches me.

"Not a creature was stirring, not even a mouse."

"Why would it be stirring?" Aidan asks incredulously. Cade chuckles, explaining the different definitions of stirring as both kids listen with rapt attention.

As the story goes on, Rylin starts to sink lower, her head nearly resting on Cade's thigh when she yawns. I pull her legs onto my lap and cover her with a blanket, watching her eyelids grow heavy.

"Happy Christmas to all, and to all a good night!"

Liam shuffles out of his spot on the floor, picking up a sleepy Aidan. "Bedtime, buddy. Say thank you to Uncle Cade."

"Sanks Uncle Cade," he says through a yawn. "Night."

"Night bud," Cade says, offering his hand in a fist bump.

A soft snore comes out of the sleeping toddler on Cade's lap as he strokes a hand over her curls. "I should get Rylin to bed, too," Ivy says.

Before she can stand, Cade shifts her into his arms instead. "I've got her."

"Thanks," she says. He stops in front of her so she can kiss her girl goodnight, then disappears up the stairs. Silence stretches, the only sound in the room emanating from the fireplace.

"So, what do we do now?" Ivy asks.

"Would you rather?" Miles suggests.

"That could be fun! We can make it a Christmas edition," Cara adds. "Who goes first?"

Cade sits down beside me, placing a mug of cocoa in my hand as Liam retakes his seat on the floor. I moan around the cup as the warm chocolate hits my tongue, and Cade groans under his breath. Pulling me into his side, he whispers in my ear. "Keep making noises like that and I'm gonna have to carry you up the stairs, too, baby."

"Don't tempt me with a good time," I tease, nipping at his bottom lip.

He fists my hair, bringing his lips to my ear again before tugging on the lobe. "Be a good girl and I'll take care of you later."

"Ugh. Can you not?" Mags snorts playfully. "I'm gonna need you to leave at least a foot of space between you for the rest of the night. Actually. You know what..." she trails off, standing from her spot on the sofa before shoving us apart and squeezing in between us.

"Much better." My best friend rolls her eyes dramatically and shrugs as Cade narrows his eyes at her. "Sorry, Cowboy. I need quality bestie time and you're hogging her."

Miles snickers as he watches the scene unfold. "I guess I'll go first," he says. "Would you rather wrap 100 presents or untangle 20 strands of Christmas lights?"

"100% wrapping presents," I say. "Tangled Christmas lights are a nightmare and there's no guarantee they actually work when you're done with them."

There's not much of a debate until Ivy chimes in. "You can wrap my presents all day," she says. "I hate it."

"Ok Paige, you're up," Miles says, tipping his mug in my direction.

I contemplate my options for a while — this game is exponentially harder when it has a theme. "Would you rather receive eleven pipers piping or twelve drummers drumming?"

"Can we ask follow-up questions?" Dean asks, gesturing to Miles, who's taken on the role of moderator for our little game.

"Sure, why not," Miles confirms with a shrug.

"Alright. Are they continuously piping and drumming?" he asks.

"Yes," I clarify, resting my head on Maggie's shoulder with a sigh. It's getting late and I'm exhausted from the day's excitement.

"Harsh. I'll go with the drummers," Dean says, pulling a tired-looking Cara into his side. "I feel like they could at least tone it down a little when it gets annoying. I could handle a subtle drumroll." Everyone agrees with Dean's assessment and the next round falls to him.

"Would you rather give a lap dance to a mall Santa, or do a striptease at the work Christmas party?" Cara snorts into her drink and slaps Dean on the chest.

"I better not hear about you doing a striptease at the work Christmas party," she says. "I don't think Khaki Ken in I.T. would survive." Snorts of laughter erupt around the room, but they're halfhearted — it seems we're all feeling the effects of a full day of excitement. I'll admit, I've had a blast, but we're not kids anymore and I'm growing an entire human being. The fatigue is definitely setting in.

I'm just about to choose the strip tease since I don't actually have any employees, when the power suddenly comes back on, momentarily blinding us all. "Jesus," Cade winces at the sudden onslaught, bringing his arm up to cover his eyes. "I think that's our queue to call it a night."

After saying goodnight, we all go our separate ways. Taking the stairs feels like a chore as I drag my ass up to bed. Cade slaps me on the ass. "Get a move on. I have plans for you." A shiver crawls up my spine and suddenly, I'm not tired in the least.

Chapter 8

Mags

♫ *Kiss Me At Midnight - NSYNC*

The house is quiet as I slide out of bed, careful not to wake Ivy. The Christmas tree lights sparkle, guiding my way down the stairs. There's another dim light in the kitchen and my body tenses, anticipating the worst. Miles fucking Barlow. Dear Gods, what did I ever do to deserve this karma?

He's leaning up against the countertop in a pair of low slung gray sweatpants and nothing else. I can clearly see the outline of his above average cock as he eyes me across the island. "Eyes are up here, Wildcat."

Averting my gaze, I ignore the irritating nickname and start the kettle. If I know Paige, she's got a whole stash of tea here somewhere. I open drawers in search of the box with the little bear on it. By the 3rd one, I'm losing hope until I look up and there it is, on the open shelving just above the plates. Fuck. I reach an arm up and jump, but it's no use. These high ceilings aren't made for my 5ft nothing frame. I'm just about to pull over the stool when Miles slides in beside me, his solid chest brushing against my shoulder as he reaches for the box.

My breath hitches as he hands it over, our fingertips brushing in a featherlight touch. "Thanks," I say, keeping my tone curt. Why the fuck does my body react to him this way? It's not even that he can coax a reaction from me, it's that he's the only one who can. Believe me, I've tried.

We're way too fucking close and he smells amazing — fresh, like sage mixed with something else I can't quite place. Miles' eyes flick to my lips and I abruptly turn away as the kettle clicks off. He chuckles behind my back and the sound goes straight to my pussy. No. Nope. Not gonna happen.

I find the biggest mug on the shelf, double bagging the steamy water. If I don't get my ass to sleep, I'm going to do something reckless. "Mags," my name on his lips makes my stomach do a flip, and I don't think it's ever sounded so... gentle. "I think we should talk," he says.

"What's there to talk about? I said all I needed to say a long time ago."

I walk towards the den with my tea in hand. "There's something you should know," he starts, but I turn on my heel, cutting him off with a finger on his lips. If I had any kind of foresight, I would've noticed where I stopped — directly under the fucking mistletoe. Not again.

Miles nips at the pad of my finger, causing my nipples to pebble beneath my barely there sleep shirt. He reaches out, sliding an errant lock of hair behind my ear. "It wasn't —" Before he can finish his sentence, I rise onto my tiptoes, lightly brushing my lips against his stubbled cheek, but my trajectory is off and I brush the corner of his mouth. It's not a heated kiss. In fact, it barely meets the definition of one. I just hope it satisfies whatever sadistic forces are torturing me like this. His nostrils flare as I scoot past him into the den, ignoring the wounded look in his eyes — Not for the first time.

I don't see Miles again that night, and the tea does its job. I wake the next morning with an orange cat making biscuits on my chest, and a pair of brown eyes boring into the side of my head.

"Good morning, Sunshine." My voice is gravelly, and my eyes are blurry as I adjust to the morning light flooding the room. With the snow on the ground, it's overly bright.

"What did you do to Miles?" she questions, and shit, she's mad.

I scoot my butt up the couch, propping myself against a plethora of throw pillows. I take note of the knit blanket covering my lap. My brow furrows — I didn't put that there. "I don't know what you're talking about."

"Oh, really? Then why is he walking around the house like someone shit in his shoes?"

"I don't know. Maybe Goose here shit in his shoes," I chortle, stroking the purring menace who's taken up residence on my lap.

"It's not funny, Mags. Whatever shit y'all have going on needs to be resolved."

"That's the thing. It is resolved. We've resolved to steer clear of each other. It's not my fault my best friend married his best friend. Honestly, you could've been a little more considerate."

Paige rolls her eyes and huffs out a laugh. "I love you, Mags. But sometimes I hate you."

"No, you don't."

"No. I don't," she concedes.

Miles

Waking up with a hard cock for the 2nd night in a row wouldn't be so bad if I didn't have to sleep on the floor in the laundry room. The only other option was to slide in beside Ivy, and that definitely isn't happening. Don't get me wrong, Ivy's a great girl and gorgeous as hell, but she's not my type. What is my type, you ask? Not to be too specific, but a 5ft pixie with long brown hair, deep chocolate eyes that turn black when she glares at me, a tight fucking body that makes my dick stand at attention just thinking about it, and absolutely, unequivocally hates my guts.

In my defense, I don't mean to antagonize her — it just comes naturally. And she gives as good as she gets. That woman is a fucking nightmare, but she's also the star of all my wet dreams. I stroke a hand over my sweatpants, trying to ease the ache, but it's no use. There's only one way to cure what ails me and it's gonna have to be my fist. I rise quietly, making sure not to wake Mags, who's asleep in the den, which is directly in my path to the bathroom.

She's beautiful like this, her hair spread over the pillows with a hand under her cheek; she's curled up under the blanket I draped over her shortly after she fell asleep, and the thought of being able to care for her does something to me. She'd never in a million years accept any genuine affection from me, so I'll keep that memory locked away for myself.

I tiptoed past my wildcat, nearly crashing into Paige on the way to the bathroom. I try to hide the unease that's likely written all over my face, but it's too late. "You good?"

"Yeah. Just gonna go shower."

She stops me with a hand on my forearm, a look of concern on her face. "Miles —"

"I'm fine, Sunshine. Just tired."

"Ok," she sighs. She doesn't believe me, but I know she

won't push. She's good like that — always there if you need to talk, but she'll let you take that step. Cade and Dean have been my best friends for as long as I can remember, but as soon as we met Paige, she became one of us.

I'm not sure what I'm gonna do with a baby joining our crew — "Uncle Miles" doesn't sound too bad, though. Matt, my younger brother, is 22 years old and still partying through his 20s. He's in no place to settle down anytime soon. On top of that, he has a lot of shit to atone for where I'm concerned. No. I won't be a biological uncle anytime soon. But Cade is more of a brother to me than Matty ever was. There's also Aidan and Rylin who might as well be family, too.

I reach the downstairs bathroom without further incident. It's a smaller space with a stand up shower, but no less beautiful compared to the rest of the cabin, with its sage green tiles and gold fixtures to match the rest of the house. I scan the space, admiring my own work — Cade hired Barlow Constructions for the remodel, so I'm a little biased.

I turn the shower to frigid, trying anything to ease the ache in my balls. How long has it been since I've sunk into something warm and wet? *Too goddamn long.*

Every attempt at dick control goes right out the window when I come out of the bathroom and nearly run into Mags wearing nothing but her tiny pajamas. She's mussed from sleep and fuck if she doesn't look like she just had marathon sex. Rock hard seems to be my default setting whenever Mags is around.

"Oof. Fuck. Shit. Dammit." The riot of curses coming from her mouth is amusing, to say the least.

"Woah there, sailor. You good?" Mags glares up at me

through her thick lashes, sending a jolt of electricity through my veins. She clenches her fists and rests them on her hips, trying to appear intimidating, and I guess it might work — if I were a mouse. I smirk down at her, taking a step into her personal space. I'm well aware that I'm playing with fire, but fuck if I don't want to get burned. "What's wrong, wildcat?"

Maggie's eyes follow a drop of water as it trails down my chest to my belly button, disappearing into my towel. "See something you like?"

"Nope. No. Fuck no." She stammers, her eyes darting around the narrow hallway, finally stopping on a wall sconce. "Get out of my way, Miles."

I smirk as she she shoves past me into the bathroom. She might think she hates me, but her body's reaction tells me there's something else she's keeping buried beneath the surface. What's the saying? There's a fine line between love and hate. Mark my words, someday soon Maggie Watson is going to find out what it feels like to cross it.

Chapter 9

Liam

♫ *Santa Can't You Hear Me*
- Kelly Clarkson & Ariana Grande

Sipping my coffee, the morning light streams in through the picture window at the front of the house, casting its light on the new dusting of snow we received overnight. Paige joins Cade on the sofa with a wistful sigh. He kisses her forehead in that disgustingly sweet way he does and she practically melts into a puddle. She smiles up at him, contentedly snuggling deeper into his hold.

"Hmmm. Think we should tackle some more of your list?" he asks.

Paige perks up at that. "What do you have in mind?" she asks.

Cade shrugs. "Any ideas?"

A thought pops into my head as I recall what's left of Paige's list. "If everyone's up for another trek outside. I have a score to settle with Cara."

As if summoned out of thin air, Cara and Dean walk into

the den hand in hand, her narrowed eyes boring into mine. "Oh, it's on, Scrooge!" she says.

Another snowball soars past me and Aidan as he clings to my back like a koala bear. "Run dad, faster!"

Paige is walking around the yard with a camera in hand, taking pictures of the battlefield as

I duck behind a tree, pausing to consider our next move. Aidan hops down off my back, setting to work on a small pile of snowballs. "I say we bide our time and hit 'em when they least expect it," I say.

"Yeah. They won't know what hit 'em." My mini me holds out his hand for a fist bump, then blows it up on impact. "Let's do this." This kid has so much of me in him, it's crazy to think I've only had him for less than 2 years. I'm so goddamn proud to call him mine.

Before we can enact our grand plan, a snowball is smashed over my head, melting down the back of my jacket. "You're gonna pay for that, Carebear," I say, stalking after her in the ankle deep snow. She's fast, but I was a pitcher in high school and my aim is still second to none as my snowball connects with the center of her back. I waste no time tossing another and Aidan joins in as she cages her head between her elbows, protecting her face and neck from the onslaught.

A chorus of giggles distracts me just long enough for Cara to get away, as Rylin runs as fast as her little legs will carry her. She's b-lining for Aidan, with Ivy hot on her heels. "Help!" she squeals, and my boy wraps her in his arms, shielding her from her mom. Ivy's eyes turn glassy as she stops in her tracks, taking in the sight, and I have to admit it's damn cute. I never gave much thought to having kids until Aidan showed up, but I'd give anything to go back in time. It pains me that I missed the first 5 years of his life.

I put myself in Ivy's path, shielding our kids from the impending attack. "Whaddaya say we combine forces and take the fight to Dean and Cara?" I suggest.

"What's in it for me?" She quirks a brow. I'll admit that Ivy is hot as fuck, and back in the day I would've been all over that, but I only have eyes for... someone else. Someone completely off-limits, so I'm destined to spend my nights fucking my fist to thoughts of her honey blonde hair fanned out on the pillows; the soft swells of her tits rising and falling with every stuttered breath as I bury my head between her thick thighs. Snap the fuck out of it, Liam.

"I'll owe you one. You name it."

"Hmmmm. Intriguing." She scans her surroundings, taking in any potential threats as we've been standing out in the open for a while. "Fine. You've got yourself a deal, Irish."

"Alright, fine. You won this time," Cara harrumphs from her spot on the sectional, her feet in Dean's lap as he massages the feeling back into her toes. It was a close one. They tried to force a mutiny, but my crew was loyal to the end, leaving Cara and Dean outnumbered. We returned to the house with frozen extremities and hungry bellies. Aidan immediately disappeared into the kitchen with Cade and Paige, as I sunk down onto the plush sofa.

"How are you holding up?" Ivy asks. "You've done more talking today than I've heard from all year — you must be exhausted," she smirks.

I shake my head and flip her the bird. "I'm just happy Aidan's having a good time. And, to be honest, we both needed this break." Ivy nods as something sullen passes over her features. I don't have time to ask her about it as Aiden and Rylin come barreling into the room.

They plop down on the floor in front of the coffee table, bouncing in anticipation as Paige sets out a massive platter of finger foods — everything from dinosaur chicken nuggets to pigs in a blanket. It's every kid's dream, and honestly, it looks damn good to me, too.

With the kids distracted by food, I take the opportunity to check in with Ivy. I know she's been going through a lot, but she doesn't talk about it and I'm concerned. "How's everything with the ex?"

She cringes at the mention of Rylin's dad. "Same shit, different pile." Her flippant response is betrayed by her downcast eyes.

I watch her warily for a moment. "You ever need me to..." I trail off, letting the subtle homicidal insinuation hang in the air. I might not be much of a talker, and I've been told I can be downright broody sometimes, but I'm loyal to a fucking fault and nothing gets me more riled up than a man who thinks it's okay to hurt a woman.

"Thanks, Li." With a nod, she sips her cocoa, letting the silence stretch.

Chapter 10

Mags

♫ *What Christmas Means to Me - Hanson*

I swear we're all going to be made up entirely of hot cocoa and frozen extremities by the time we're free to leave this place. Paige is sipping from yet another ridiculous novelty mug as she scans her updated list.

"Ready to check off another one?" I ask, scanning the paper over her shoulder.

"Yeah, but I'm so over being outside. Maybe we should skip to the gingerbread houses," she suggests.

"You had me at gingerbread. Let's get baking, then we can rally the troops."

I busy myself around the kitchen, gathering everything we need for the project. Half an hour later, the island is strewn with a haphazard mix of supplies as Paige frantically tries to make sense of the disarray. "Babe, why don't you get started on the cookies and I'll organize?"

She sighs. "Thank fuck. My brain is too overwhelmed for this."

"What's going on in here?" I startle at the sudden intrusion, a bag of gumdrops scattering to the floor.

"Fucking hell, Miles."

"My bad." To my utter shock, Miles rounds the island, crouching down to help me pick up the mess. His proximity unsettles me and I'm so distracted by his presence, I miss the moment we reach for the same piece of candy, his fingertips brushing against mine, sending a jolt of electricity through me. I recoil at his touch, and he jumps back like I've slapped him.

"Sorry," he says, quickly retreating to the other side of the counter, putting several feet of distance between us.

"Hey Miles," Paige cuts in. "What are the odds your construction experience could help with gingerbread houses?" Paige asks. "This is all a bit confusing."

Miles' face lights up with his signature smirk. "Say less. I was born for this," he says, snatching up the wax paper as he quickly draws out several templates for the cookie pieces. Even I can admit, it's impressive as fuck to watch him free handing the whole design.

"Very mid century modern," Cade jokes, leaning against the counter beside his wife.

"Don't harass my contractor, Cowboy," Paige says. "Why don't you make yourself useful and preheat the oven?"

"Mmm... you didn't complain about my usefulness last night," he says, giving her a little tap on the ass as he pushes past her to the oven.

Miles snickers as he steps back to admire his work. "There. Now you just have to roll out the dough and cut around the templates. How many are we making?"

"I'm thinking we team up. Me and Cade, Ivy and Rylin, Liam and Aidan, Cara and Dean —"

My eyes go wide as I calculate her next words. "I'mma stop you right there. I'll work alone."

Miles seems to have come to the same conclusion as he

smirks at me from across the island. "What's wrong, Wildcat? Afraid you won't be able to keep up?"

"Pfft. You wish. I just don't feel like teaming up with a jackass."

He clutches his heart, stumbling backwards with a smirk. "Ouch. That stings."

"Alright, quit pissing off my bestie, Barlow," Paige says. "Mags and Miles will make separate gingerbread houses on one condition." We both eye her cautiously from opposite ends of the kitchen. "No more bickering. You two need to get the fuck over whatever bullshit you have going on for the rest of Maggie's trip." I groan at her admonishment.

"I can behave myself if she can," Miles snickers.

I roll my eyes in response. "My god, you're such a child sometimes."

"See what I mean? You two can't even just agree to be civil. Behave or get the fuck out of my kitchen." It's been a long time since I've seen Paige quite so irritated, and I'm feeling suitably scolded.

Cade wraps Paige in his arms, murmuring something in her ear that has her blushing as Miles and I come to a silent agreement. I don't know how long this truce will last, but I'm not about to get on Paige's bad side while we're all cooped up in this cabin for at least another day. *Good vibes only, Mags.*

The spicy sweet scents of gingerbread and frosting fill the air as I set the last bowl of candy on the island. All the pieces are baked and ready for assembly, and I can admit that Miles' templates worked perfectly, much to my annoyance. The piping bags are filled, and the candy is separated and spread out in bowls along the counter, and each team's station is prepped with a cardboard base.

Everyone claims a spot, and when all is said and done, I'm unfortunately seated right next to Miles. My first attempt at assembly is an utter disaster as I struggle to keep the walls upright. It all turns to complete shit when it crumbles for a 3rd time, with one wall snapping entirely in half. Instead of soldiering on, I take a moment to pout and nibble on one corner of my apparently load-bearing wall. "At least it tastes good, I guess," I scoff, shaking myself out of the disappointment as Miles effortlessly places his roof.

"Come here, Wildcat." His tone is gentle, almost hesitant, as he tugs my stool closer to him. "I'm good with construction, but I have a feeling I'll need your expertise for the decor."

His kindness catches me off guard, and I'm fighting the urge to resist his invitation. But this activity was my idea, and I'll admit I'm more than a little excited to come up with a design.

"Here," he says, passing me a piping bag and a bowl of gumdrops. "The roof, maybe?"

Unable to hold myself back, I set to work piping a line of frosting down the center of the roof, following along with a row of red and green alternating gumdrops. A smile blooms on my face as I continue down the panel, making a scallop pattern to mimic roofing tiles then covering them in a sprinkling of powdered sugar for a dusting of snow.

I meet Paige's gaze across the island and she shrugs, glancing down at her gingerbread house. As her disastrous creation comes into focus, we both burst into laughter. "Holy shit, Paige. That's terrible," I say through tears of amusement.

"In my defense, Cade doesn't have a creative bone in his body," she says.

"Oh, I have a bone for you, alright," he says, smearing frosting on her nose before licking it off. Miles chucks a

64

gumdrop across the space, hitting Cade square in the forehead. Rylin's giggles fill the room as she joins in the fray and lobs her own gumdrops at Cade.

"Go Ry!" Miles says, encouraging the chaos.

"Miles Barlow," Ivy scolds, tossing a fistful of sprinkles at him. "Stop encouraging my daughter to throw her food."

"Pot meet kettle, Ivy Jo," Paige says, hitting Ivy in the boob with a peppermint.

The whole scene devolves into a massive food fight, our gingerbread houses all but forgotten. By the time we're out of ammunition, everyone is covered in a mixture of powdered sugar, frosting, and candy.

I sink down onto a stool, snatching a frosting covered piece of gingerbread. "Not quite the redemption I was hoping for," I say, biting into my treat.

Miles' deep chuckle reverberates through me, causing a flutter to erupt in my chest, as the rest of our friends retreat to the various rooms to get cleaned up. He snatches the piece of paper off the fridge and pulls out a pen, striking through the gingerbread line item, replacing it with "food fight" and quickly checking it off.

"Problem solved," he says, before leaving me alone with a belly full of butterflies and a very inconvenient lady boner. *Problem definitely not solved.*

SNOW MUCH FUN

Paige's Holiday Bucket List

0 stars, do not recommend

- ⊗ Sledding ~~(call archie)~~
- ✓ Visit tree farm
- ✓ Snowball fight
- ✓ Hot Cocoa
- ○ Snow angels
- ✓ Secret santa
- ○ Build a snowman
- ○ Mistletoe kisses
- ✓ *FOOD FIGHT* ~~Gingerbread redemption~~

Pizzelles!!

xoxo Mags

Chapter 11

Ivy

♫ *Snow Angel - Elli Moore*

"Auntie Paige, you gots carrots?" Rylin asks, bouncing up and down on the balls of her feet, her tiny body vibrating with glee.

"Hmmm," she replies, exaggerating the sound with a contemplative gesture for my daughter's benefit. "Why don't we check the fridge?" She holds out a hand for Rylin to take, then leads her into the kitchen. I watch as they disappear out of the den with a wistful sigh.

If I'm being honest, I was starting to doubt we'd ever have this. The people in this house have brought more happiness to our life than I ever thought possible. Everyone has welcomed me with open arms, and Rylin now has a whole crew of aunts and uncles to dote on her. There's still so much of our future that's uncertain, but I won't dwell on any of that now.

Rylin comes running back into the room with a huge carrot in her tiny fist. "What's this for, love?"

"Wanna make a snowman!" she says excitedly. Paige smiles

68

back at me and I glance around at our friends, wondering if they're up for another outdoor adventure so soon.

"Come on, Ry. Aidan. Let's get your gear on," Liam says, taking my daughter by the hand as Aidan follows them to the coat rack.

Cara and Dean decide to stay in and watch a movie, and Mags has a video call with her dad in Aspen while the rest of our crew heads out to the front yard to start the snowman assembly. As soon as we step outside, Miles dashes to the freshly powdered driveway and plops down on his back, moving his arms and legs around to make a snow angel.

Rylin giggles as she watches the scene unfold. "Uncle Miles, you silly!" she says. "Me too?" She looks up at me. Her little nose is red and her expression is hopeful.

"Have at it, sweet girl."

With an excited yip, my girl plops down beside Miles, his snow angel dwarfing hers in the most adorable way as she spreads her arms and legs in a much less coordinated fashion.

"Come on, Mommy!" she says, her little hands beckoning me to join them. I could never deny her this simple request. I fall to my ass beside her and she beams at me as I create my own snow angel. It looks like a little family, and another part of my heart shatters as memories of the past come flooding back. This is everything I ever wanted, and it's not even mine. No matter how much I try to convince myself that I'm enough for her, there's another part of me that knows there will always be something missing.

The holidays were always a nightmare with Austin. I'd pour my heart and soul into making all the Christmas magic for our family, and he would sit back and sneer. He never made an effort and not once in all the years we were together did he ever give me anything meaningful. Most holidays and birthdays were all but forgotten.

"Hey. You okay?" Liam's voice snaps me back to reality as the snow starts to seep through my clothing.

"Shit. Yeah. Help me up?" Liam holds out a hand, pulling me to standing and I almost wish I could feel something more than friendship for him. I have no doubt he'll make a wonderful partner someday. That's just not in the cards for me.

Paige approaches with a basket full of snowman accessories with a hint of mischief in her eyes.

"I think we should make this a little more interesting."

"What'd you have in mind?" Liam asks.

"Snowman contest. We break off into teams. Cara, Dean, and Mags can vote on a winner. Miles, you're with me and Cade. Liam and Ivy, you get the kids. If you add them together, they're like 10 years old, which basically adds up to a Miles."

Miles snorts out a laugh. "That's fair."

As snowflakes dance around us, the thrill of competition takes over. "Okay, team! We've got to make the best snowman ever!" I say, glancing at Liam, Rylin, and Aidan. Rylin squeals with excitement, her cheeks flushed from the cold, while Aidan's eyes sparkled with determination.

"Let's give him a cool scarf and a big carrot nose!" Aidan suggests, kneeling down to pack the snow tightly. Once he's gathered a good sized ball, he starts to crawl across the yard, rolling the ball along to increase its size.

"And we need to make him look friendly," I say, jabbing a grumpy Liam in the ribs, spurring him into action. He picks up a few twigs, examining them as potential arms.

My girl bends down, mimicking Aidan, though her snowball is a little more lopsided by the end of her first trek through the snow.

Liam chuckles from behind me. "Should've known they'd use Cade's cowboy hat." His eyes are fixed on the competition, and I have to admit, their snowman looks pretty impressive.

"Ours will be the cutest!" Aidan says. God, I love this kid; his lighthearted spirit is infectious. We pack more snow and fashion a somewhat lopsided but lovable snow woman, draping a bright yellow scarf around her neck. Aidan places 2 mismatched rocks where the eyes would be, as Liam hoists Rylin up to place the crooked carrot nose in the center of the face. We've run out of accessories, so I swipe a finger through the face, creating an indentation for a smile. It looks more like a smirk, but it does the trick.

When I glance over, Paige and Cade are securing a red bandana around their cowboy's neck and Miles is breaking off a branch for arms. Rylin stands at my side, eyeing our creation with a furrowed brow. "What's wrong, Ry?" Liam asks.

"Need a hat," she says matter-of-factly. Before I can respond, she's running over to Miles, tugging on his pant leg. He crouches down to her level with a sweet smile on his face as she leans in to whisper in his ear. With a chuckle, Miles removes the bright pink "Fuck the Patriarchy" hat, handing it over to my girl with a wink. She hugs him tightly round the neck, and the big ol' softie melts.

Rylin runs over to us with a look of pure joy on her face. My girl could talk her way out of purgatory if given the chance. I think it's the big blue eyes. Taking the hat from her hands, I place it atop the snowman. "Perfect!"

Paige

Ok, I can admit we had a bit of an advantage on our team, but they did a damn good job. Our snow cowboy is cute as fuck, but even I would give the win to Ivy's team.

"Miles! Are you playing for the other team?" I chastise.

"Hey now! I was coerced," he says. "Have you ever been

confronted by a little girl with big, sad blue eyes? I was helpless."

"And what exactly did she whisper in your ear?" Ivy asks, a smug expression on her face.

"She said I'm her favorite. What can I say? Kids got good taste."

I shake my head. "Who amongst us hasn't fallen victim to Rylin's baby blues?"

"Ok. I'm gonna head in to grab the judges," Cade declares, leaving me with a kiss on the cheek. He returns several minutes later with Cara, Dean, and Mags in tow. "They've been briefed. They'll each give a score out of 10. The team with the most points wins."

All three judges circle the creations, playing up their assessments for the benefit of the kids. They murmur to each other in silly accents, Rylin and Aidan giggling as they take in the scene.

"I say," Mags says in an exaggerated English accent. "Jolly good, this is. This here's a cheeky one."

"True, mate. This one's a bit serious for a snowman, don't ya reckon?" Cara adds. Her hilarious Australian accent leaves a lot to be desired. "A cowboy? In the dead of winter?"

"Aye," Dean says with a thick Scottish accent. "I cannae help but admire that wee snow lassie. She's got a charm that just draws ye in, doesn't she?"

I'm grinning from ear to ear, watching my friends put on a show for the little ones. Rylin's bouncing up and down as they praise her creation and she's absolutely beaming. What I wouldn't give to bottle some of that joy. It hits me then that I'll have one of my own this time next year. I can't fucking wait. I wrap an arm around Cade's waist, leaning up to place a kiss on his stubble.

Once they've finished scribbling on their notepads, the judges hold up scores ranging from 8 to 9.5 for the Cowboy snowman while the "lassie" as she's been deemed gets a perfect score of 10 from every judge. Rylin whoops and throws herself into Ivy's arms. "We did it, mommy! We winned!"

"Sure did, sweet girl! Couldn't have done it without you."

"Best snowman ever," Aidan declares.

"You rig the game, Cowboy?" I smirk up at my husband.

"You would've done the same thing, don't even deny it," he says. "I just gave them a little nudge. But I think this would've been the outcome, regardless."

"You're gonna be a wonderful dad, Cade Brooks."

He smiles down at me, and if I were a snowman, I'd melt.

"Only one thing left on the list," Cade says, as he checks off another item. I smirk, knowing exactly what I have planned for that last activity.

After the snowman contest, we made a quick lunch and most of the crew headed off to their rooms to change and warm up. "Looks like everyone can get out of here in the morning. We have the holiday party at The Ridge in 3 days, and while I love my friends, I'm ready to get you alone." His voice is dripping with desire as his arms circle my waist. His lips find my collarbone, causing a shiver.

"Mmm. You had me alone last night, Cowboy."

"I need to hear you screaming my name, Mrs. Brooks." His hand finds my neck and I moan at the same time Miles walks in on the scene.

His eyes practically bug out of his head as he registers our position behind the kitchen island. "Jesus. Get a room."

"Funny. I thought this was a room," Cade deadpans.

"Get a different one. Preferably with a door. And maybe a

lock. And judging by what I heard last night, probably some sound proofing."

"Miles!"

"Don't worry, Sunshine. It's nothing I haven't heard a million times before. But it's usually, "Yes, Miles", "Harder, Miles", "Your dick is so big, Miles.""

"More like, "Shut the fuck up, Miles," Mags says with an eye roll as she hops up onto a stool. I'm not a mind reader, but I'd guess Mags is pretty excited about the idea of the roads being cleared by morning, too.

Chapter 12

Paige

♫ *Secret Santa - Twinnie*

As I step out of the cabin, the crisp air fills my lungs, energizing me to venture into town after days of being cooped up. The sun peeks through the clouds, casting a soft glow on the remnants of snow that's blanketing the town. I tighten my scarf around my neck, smiling as Cade steps out behind me, boxes lined with packaged pizzelles balanced carefully in his arms. I've been looking forward to visiting our friends around town. Sharing pizzelles had always been a huge part of Nana's Christmas traditions, and I always wanted to carry it on with my own family.

Snow crunches softly underfoot as we head out to the truck, the scent of pine lingering in the air. Cade places the boxes into the back of the truck, then holds out a hand to help me into the passenger side, securing my buckle with a kiss to my temple. We hit the road with my list of names in hand.

I decided it was probably best to start with the furthest

destination, then make our way back. As we turn the corner onto a familiar dirt road, passing the sign for Whispering Oaks Ranch, a sense of peace settles over me. For the past several years, our family Christmases have been rife with tension and drama. It feels good to finally let all of that go.

The sound of horses whinnying in the distance fills the silence as I knock on the door of the familiar white farmhouse. Evelyn appears on the threshold, her eyes lighting up when she realizes who's standing on her doorstep. I'm immediately engulfed in her warm, motherly hug as she pulls me into her arms. "What are y'all doing here?"

"I come bearing gifts," I say, as she releases me from her hold. "These are my Nana's pizzelles. It's always been something of a tradition to share them with the people we love."

Evie's eyes crinkle as she smiles back at me, taking the package from my hands. "Thank you, sweet girl. Do you wanna come in?"

"Wish we could, but we've got a helluva lotta these packages to deliver," Cade says with a chuckle. "Good to see you, Evie."

"You too. Y'all come by for dinner one of these days, alright?" She pulls me into another hug then narrows her eyes at Cade, "And you better be taking good care of your girls."

"Yes, ma'am."

We make our way back, stopping at a few houses along the way before pulling up to the curb outside of Rosie's. The bell jingles as I push through the door, and the rich aroma of comfort food fills the air. Rosie and Archie are in their usual spot at the end of the counter, sharing a slice of pecan pie when we approach.

"Well hey there, my girl," Archie says, pulling me into a side hug. "Bet you're happy to be out and about after that storm. Haven't seen anything like it in years. 'Cept maybe that ice storm last year."

Cade shivers beside me, recalling the memory of the storm that kept us apart for a week. "It wasn't so bad. Gave me some time to get a lot of baking done." I hold out the bag for Rosie, and she beams at me.

"Oh, Paige! You are a ray of sunshine!" Her voice is like a warm hug. "These look delightful!"

"I had some help," I say, explaining how our 4 days of forced proximity led to all kinds of adventures. "Anyway, I thought everyone could use a little sweetness after being snowed in."

Rosie invited us to sit down for brunch and we talked over the last few days and our plans for the big holiday party at The Ridge before we said our goodbyes.

After a few more stops and cheerful exchanges, I feel somehow lighter. The town is waking up again, and I love being a part of it. I never thought I'd feel so connected to a place and to so many people. There's an overwhelming amount of heart in this town, and I can't imagine living anywhere else.

Mags

Everyone headed out bright and early this morning, so it was the perfect time for me to dive into the final chapters of my book. It's a fairytale retelling set in a small town at Christmas. My characters have been well established for months, so why do I have the sudden urge to rewrite the male love interest with blonde hair and blue eyes? Why can't I stop thinking about the feel of his body pressed up against me under the mistletoe? Why can't I leave Miles in the past where he belongs?

Tossing my pen down beside my laptop, I lean back in the chair, inhaling a steadying breath. Just as I'm about to pack up my things, Goose jumps up onto the table, begging for attention. He purrs contentedly as I stroke his head. "It's no use, buddy. I have fucking writer's block again."

"Writer's block?" A familiar voice interrupts my thoughts, and my body grows rigid. Miles eyes me curiously, a candy cane hanging out of his mouth. He sucks on it as he pulls it out of his mouth and fuck, what I wouldn't give to be that candy cane right now. "What are you writing about, wildcat?"

Fuck. My. Life.

"What the fuck are you doing here?" My reaction may be a little over the top, but I don't know how to handle the feelings he's stoking within me, mixed with the idea that my secret might get out. He pulls out the chair beside me and the scent of peppermint mixed with his musky sage surrounds me. The last thing I need is Miles Mother-Fucking Barlow in my personal space. He reaches out to pull my notepad across the surface, but I slap my hand down on his, pausing the motion. The touch has electricity surging through me.

Miles' eyes narrow as he leans in closer. "What are you hiding?"

"It's none of your business. Whatever you need, get it and then get the fuck out," I spit. He's barely a breath away and I don't miss the way his eyes momentarily snag on my lips. No. No fucking way. I'm not doing this again.

With a huff, I rise from my chair and gather my things into my tote bag, making a swift exit into the den. In true Miles fashion, he follows me out. I stop in my tracks, rounding on him. "You are so infuriating." I punctuate my words with a finger to his chest and he snatches my wrist, holding me in place. One tug and our bodies would be flush and if I'm honest, I'm running out of willpower to keep myself from kissing this man. I wish he didn't make my blood heat and my pussy clench.

"Tell me your secret and I'll let you go."

"You lost any claim on my secrets a long fucking time ago."

Miles loosens his hold on me and steps back like I've burned him, and while that is the desired effect, I can't help but feel a little guilty in the wake of it.

"You're right," he says, raking a hand through his tousled blonde hair, sincerity evident on his face. "I'll leave you to it."

Once he's out of sight, I release the breath I had been holding. There's something almost suffocating about being around Miles, even though I know I shouldn't let him affect me that way.

I retreat to the safety of Paige's library to resume writing, hoping the solitude will stoke my inspiration, but once again I'm flooded by images of Miles Barlow standing under the mistletoe, with desire written all over his face. Instead of tamping down my urges, I decide to let them flow onto the paper unrestrained.

Max's gaze sears into her skin, branding her without a single touch as shivers rack her body. The mistletoe hangs overhead like a threat and a promise all at once. She wants nothing more than to reach up and remove her mask, baring herself to him for the first time, but she can't help but wonder if he would reject her if he knew.

Daylight fades as I get lost in my story — the words finally flowing freely for the first time in months. *And you have Miles to thank for that.*

The thought is unwelcome, so I wipe it from my thoughts, content to let the story unfold in whatever way feels right. Whether my character bears a passing resemblance to a certain blonde haired asshole is none of my business. Miles Barlow is none of my fucking business.

Chapter 13

Cade

♫ *I'll Be Your Santa Tonight - Keith Urban*

"You're so fucking beautiful." I stalk towards Paige, who's standing in front of the full-length mirror in her ridiculous candy cane bra and panty set with her hands splayed over her belly. Her expression is unreadable as her hands glide along her barely there bump. "What's wrong, Sunshine?"

"Huh?" Her gaze snaps to mine in the reflection and her eyes are slightly glassy. "Just a few new stretch marks." Oh, fuck no. No way is my girl going to feel bad about that.

I plant myself behind her, my arms encircling her waist to splay my palms over her soft skin. "You mean these?" I ask, trailing our joined hands over the place where our baby girl is growing. "These beautiful lines that tell me our baby girl is growing inside of you right now? Is that what's making you sad? Because I have to tell you, Sunshine — it's making me want to bend you over and spank that ass for ever thinking those marks are anything but perfection."

81

I trail one hand lower, sliding my fingers under the waistband of her panties. "You wet for me, baby?" She swallows thickly as my fingers glide along her pussy, her breaths coming in pants.

"Yes." Her voice is breathy and weak as I sink one finger inside, then another. Finding her clit with my thumb, I start to stroke in and out. Curling an arm back around my neck to keep herself steady, she moans, and throws her head back to my shoulder. The familiar scent of her lavender vanilla shampoo surrounds me as I kiss along her collarbone.

My other hand toys with the lace on her bra, gently rubbing over one peaked nipple. She groans on contact and I tug it down, giving me better access to her heaving tits. She's damn near spilling out of her bras these days, and it takes every bit of my self control not to take her on every surface of the house whenever I get home from work. Her body writhes as I pull her closer to the edge, both hands working now. "Oh, fuck. Cade."

"Gonna cum for me like a good girl?" I ask, knowing exactly what those words do to her.

"Yes. God." she breathes.

"Not God, baby." One hand continues to toy with her soaking wet pussy as I bring the other higher to gently wrap around her throat, squeezing just enough to let her know I'm in control, but not enough to cause any distress to her or the baby. She clenches around my fingers — so fucking close. "More," she begs.

"Come on my fingers and I promise I'll give you exactly what you need." My cock is straining behind my jeans as she shatters, nearly collapsing to the ground if it weren't for my arms keeping her in place. "Such a good girl for me. On the bed."

She follows my gruff command, glancing over her shoulder with a saucy expression. Her cheeks are flushed, and my dick is fucking weeping at the sight. Sometimes I still can't believe she's mine. *They're mine.*

Once she's propped up on the pillows, she reaches over to the nightstand, grasping something in her palm. Before I can question her about it, she drops her knees, spreading herself out like a goddamn buffet for me to feast on. I can't decide if I want to dive in headfirst or sink my cock into her over and over until she's screaming my name. I don't have to think for too long as Paige reveals what's in her hand; my naughty girl holds up a sprig of mistletoe above the apex of her thighs, inviting me to taste her.

Without a single ounce of hesitation, I shuck off my clothes and crawl between her thighs, wasting no time feasting on everything she's offering. Paige threads a hand through my hair, holding me right where she wants me as she takes her pleasure. She squirms, and I lay a stinging slap on her inner thigh, sending her careening over the edge as she comes on my tongue. So fucking sweet.

When I glance up at her, she looks well-fucked, and she's holding the mistletoe over her head with an adorable smile on her face. "Come here, Cowboy."

Paige

Cade plants one elbow on either side of my head as he takes my mouth in a searing kiss. His groans rumbling through him and into me as his cock nudges against my entrance and I ache for him to fill me — I don't have to wait long. Cade takes the mistletoe from my hand, as he makes love to me, every so often moving it to another spot on my body, kissing me delicately, reverently. It's so tender, I could cry. My heart is so fucking full for this man.

"I love you," I whisper. He takes my hand, intertwining

our fingers above my head as his mouth finds my neck and sucks, no doubt leaving a mark.

"Love you so fucking much, baby." While he continues stroking in out slowly and deeply, Cade cups the back of my head and buries his face in my curls. "So beautiful. So fucking perfect."

As my body starts the familiar climb, ready to fall into oblivion, his thrusts turn more frantic. "You feel so good, so big." He groans, the gruff sound making my pussy clench around his hard length. Growing impatient, I slide a hand down between us, circling my clit, and I come undone. Cade fucks me through it, his cock bottoming out over and over.

Before I can think twice, I push him off me, switching our positions so he's propped against the headboard. Cade smirks at me as I pull out the mistletoe, holding it above his cock before dipping down to lick him from root to tip, tasting our combined flavors.

"Goddamn, baby. Such a naughty girl."

A hum is all I can manage as I bring him to the back of my throat. I gaze up through my lashes. His head is thrown back, eyes closed as one hand fists my curls, guiding my head back down and holding me there. "Breathe through your nose." I do as I'm told as he fucks my face, using me for his pleasure. And fuck, why is that so hot?

"I'm gonna come," he growls, pulling me off him before crawling over me to release all over my breasts and belly. "Fuuuuuck."

Keeping my eyes locked on his, I dip a finger through his release and bring it to my mouth, tasting him. His expression turns feral as he pulls my lips to his in a hungry kiss. When we finally pull apart, we're a sticky, sweaty, panting mess, but his eyes are full of love.

"Don't know what I did to deserve you, but you just

fulfilled about 9 of my Christmas wishes," he says with that crinkly smile I love so much.

"Hmm.. maybe we should get to work on #10?"

Chuckling, he places a soft kiss on my temple. "We have to get ready. Party starts in an hour."

Resigning myself to my fate, I reluctantly drag my ass out of bed, mumbling curses under my breath. After I've showered and slathered my body in every conceivable lotion and serum, I get to work on my hair. It's an unruly mess since Cade ran his fingers through it, but the last thing I have time for is an unplanned wash day, so I gather it in a long side braid with a few face framing pieces before adding a few jewels along strands.

Cade's form appears behind me as I'm swiping on his favorite red lipstick. My man looks mouth watering in his gray slacks, white button down, and burgundy sweater. The sleeves are pushed as he fixes his watch band. Flutters erupt in my belly as I watch his hands work, recalling all the sinful things they've done to every inch of my body. Even after more than a year with this man, he still gives me butterflies.

"I think this is my favorite look," he says, eyeing my nearly naked form as I stand in the mirror in just my emerald green lace lingerie set.

"Hmmm. Do you think all of Oak Ridge will approve?" I say with a spin. If you had told me a year ago I'd be standing in front of this beautiful man, twirling and showing off all of my jiggly bits, I would've said you were crazy. But now — now I know he loves every single inch of this body, and I do, too. That's not to say I don't still have bad body days — I don't think that'll ever change.

Cade growls. "If you ever let anyone else see you like this, I'd have to pluck out their eyes."

"That's dark as fuck, Cowboy."

He grins at me in the mirror, then slaps my ass. "Get dressed, you menace."

Chapter 14

Cade

♫ *Like It's Christmas - Jonas Brothers*

The Ridge has never looked more festive. Paige outdid herself in every way, from the catering to the decor, and even the special guest. The space is almost unrecognizable with string lights on every surface, emerald silk tablecloths, poinsettias and greenery adorning each table. There's a massive Christmas tree near the stage where the live band is getting set up, but I only have eyes for the most beautiful thing in the room — my wife. Her deep red velvet dress hugs every dip and curve of her body, accentuating her growing bump, and if we didn't have a massive surprise for all our guests, I'd take her to the office and unwrap her like the goddamn gift she is.

"You're staring, Cowboy."

"You would be, too, if you could see yourself, baby." I pull her to me by the waist, kissing down her neck and collarbone. She groans as my lips tease her soft skin before gently pushing me away.

"Nope, not happening. I did not get all dolled up so you could ruin my makeup before anybody even arrives."

"Never said anything about your makeup," I smirk. "I could have you in the office and coming within 5 minutes without breaking a sweat and nobody would know unless they looked really closely at the telltale flush you get on your chest and cheeks."

She squirms on the spot, clenching her thighs together and I chuckle, knowing my words had the desired effect. I kiss her cheek and wink, retreating behind the bar to make her a mocktail. "You can't say shit like that and leave me hanging like this, Cade," she whines.

I slide over the red fruity concoction that looks like Christmas threw up all over it. Paige created a special drink menu for the night, including several kid and Paige friendly mocktails. We know our friends come as a package deal with their kids, and if I'm being honest, I couldn't have a Christmas party without them. They're as much my family as everyone else, and pretty soon, I'll have my own little one running around the place at Christmas. *That thought is both amazing and terrifying.*

"Daaaaamn Paige. You look like a whole snack," Miles says, stepping up to kiss my wife on the cheek. I would be jealous if I didn't know how close they've gotten — Paige is like a sister to Miles. Still, I give him a playful warning glare.

"You're not so bad yourself, Barlow. Love the green suit. Trying to impress anyone in particular?" she teases. Miles smirks until his gaze catches on something or someone behind Paige.

"Hey babe," Mags says. "Caterer wants to know where to set up the charcuterie board."

"Hey there, Sugar Plum Hottie," Miles teases. "How about I shimmy down your chimney tonight?"

"Sorry, Mr. Grinch. Your dick is two sizes too small,"

Maggie replies, a chorus of snorts erupting from the small crowd gathering around us.

I give Miles a knowing look before Paige and I head over to sort out the food situation, leaving Miles alone to stew in his thoughts. Glancing back, I notice that Maggie's wearing a dress the exact shade of Miles' suit. If I didn't see the scowl on Mags' face, I'd think they were together.

As the clock strikes 7 o'clock, the rest of our guests start streaming in. Archie and Rosie are the first to arrive, followed by the Hayes family, my niece Jemma and her husband Derek. Within minutes, the place is filled to the brim with an eclectic mix of friends and family, and Paige is practically beaming with excitement. Ivy and Liam chat excitedly near the stage, as Aidan and Rylin hold hands and twirl to Christmas songs playing on the jukebox.

As the song changes to a festive ballad, I tug Paige's hand, leading her to the makeshift dance floor. Her hand rests above my heart as I pull her to me, soaking in the feel of her in my arms. I'll never get enough of her. I could have a lifetime of moments like this and it would never be enough. Paige is everything I never knew I needed. "What are you thinking about?" she asks.

"That obvious?"

She smirks. "You've got this far off look in your eyes, and when you think really hard those 2 little lines appear right here," she says, pressing her thumb to the spot between my eyebrows, smoothing it out. "And this little dimple in your cheek deepens, too."

I raise a hand to capture hers, placing a kiss on her open palm. "Just thinking about how much I love you. Can you believe just last year we were stuck doing FaceTime over the holidays? Nana was cussing like a sailor, and your friends were interrogating you about our relationship."

Something somber passes over her features, and I instantly

regret bringing up the past. While therapy has been a huge help, she still has a lot to process, and her relationship with her parents is an open wound. But things are improving with her brother, and Nana calls once a week to check in. In many ways, I know it's not enough to erase the hurt that lingers, but I'm hoping with time she'll come to see that she has everything she needs right here.

"I wish we could've had this so much sooner," she whispers, laying her head over my heart. My hurt thunders in my chest as she continues to speak. "It seems impossible we've only been together that long, and yet I feel like I've been in love with you forever."

"We've got forever to make up for lost time, baby," I say, absentmindedly twirling one of her curls around my finger. "This time next year we'll be dancing just like this, with our baby girl between us. And the year after that, maybe another."

"Woah, hold your horses, Cowboy. I'm not quite ready for a whole brood," she snorts. "Let me get through this pregnancy first and then we'll talk about more babies. For all you know, she could be an absolute nightmare and we'll never want anymore."

"That girl is going to be half of you, Paige. She's already perfect." She glances up at me through her lashes as a tear escapes down her cheek. "Don't cry," I say, swiping it away with my thumb. "If I'm not allowed to ruin your makeup, neither are you."

She laughs, then sniffs back the unshed tears. She must see the concern written on my face because she clarifies. "Happy tears. Promise."

As the song changes to something more upbeat, we escape to the outskirts of the party. Once we're safely tucked away, Paige leans over to whisper in my ear, keeping our conversation discreet. "When does she arrive?"

I check my watch, noting the time. "She should be slipping into the office any minute. Let's go." She follows me down the dimly lit hallway just in time to see the door swinging open and the one and only Ruby Lynn Hayes slipping inside.

"Hey there, you two. How's married life?"

"Ruby!" Paige exclaims, pulling her in for a hug. "It's fantastic. Thank you so much for doing this." Ruby is a Nashville country music darling, and the youngest daughter of Evelyn and Russell Hayes. They own Whispering Oaks Ranch and Ruby performed at our wedding last year. She was more than happy to do us this favor, as long as we promised to keep it a secret until she arrived.

"It's my pleasure. I was snowed in at the ranch all week so I've been itching to get out and play. How do you wanna do this?"

"Paige and I will surround you and we'll sneak along the far left wall, where she has a backdrop behind the catering table. That should give us enough cover to get you to the stage. I'll say a little something and then introduce you as our special guest. Just give Liam a signal if you need anything while you're up there, water, drinks, you name it."

At the mention of Liam's name, her gaze softens. I don't know their history, but Ruby dated his brother, Connor, in high school, and Liam's the one who asked her to perform at our wedding, so there's at least a friendship there.

"Got it. Ready when you are, boss man."

I chuckle at the nickname all of the Ridge employees have given me, assuming she caught wind of it from Liam, then lead Paige and Ruby out into the bar. The music is a dull throb beneath the loud chatter and clinking of glasses as we sneak behind the 8 foot backdrop. Our party guests are none the wiser as I step onto the stage and signal Liam to switch from the jukebox to the microphone.

"If I could have everyone's attention, please." The room

goes silent as all eyes turn to the stage. "First, I want to thank you all for being here. There's nothing more important than family, whether you were born into it, or chose it yourself. Your friendship is the greatest gift I could ever hope for this holiday season. Each person in this room is invaluable to me in some way; no one more so than my wife, Paige. I love you, baby. Thank you for putting this party together, but most of all, thank you for existing." Paige glances at me with tears in her eyes and her hands over her heart. "Without further ado, I'd like to bring up a special guest this evening. Please give a warm round of applause for the one, the only, Ruby Lynn Hayes." I step off the stage and pull my wife into my arms, careful not to mess with her makeup as I kiss her reverently.

Applause and cheers break out around the room the moment Ruby takes the stage, smiling and waving at Aidan and Rylin, who are bouncing up and down on the spot and pointing. Liam lifts an excited Aidan into his arms as the first notes of 'All I Want for Christmas is You' start playing. Not to be outdone, Rylin demands the same treatment from Uncle Miles, who tosses her gently in the air before securing her to his hip, an amused Ivy looking on.

Liam watches Ruby attentively as she strums her guitar, turning the pop hit into a country classic. A very tipsy Mags and Cara dance along and sing at the top of their lungs as Dean sips on his drink with a bemused expression. It's a heady feeling, being so surrounded by loved ones and perfectly content with where my life is right now, when this time last year, I felt aimless and unsteady.

Paige leans back into my chest, as I rock us back and forth, the music shifting to a ballad, my arms around her shoulders and her hands on mine. "Merry Christmas, Sunshine," I whisper.

Paige

The air whooshes from my lungs as I step out of The Ridge, Cade's hand clutching mine as our heads tilt up to the sky. Our friends step around us, each one gasping at the sight overhead.

Cascading swirls of pinks, purples, greens and blues light up the night sky. The northern lights aren't a common occurrence here, and though they're somewhat muted in Oak Ridge, the view is no less wondrous. I lean my head on Cade's shoulder, soaking in the silence as our loved ones surround us.

It feels like the perfect conclusion to a wonderful week. Despite a few hiccups along the way, I couldn't have dreamed up a better way to spend my first Christmas with Cade. My eyes light up as bright as the night sky, as flutters erupt in my belly.

Tears cling to my lashes as it happens again. "Oh my god," I gasp. "She's kicking." Cade places his hand over mine, and though I know he won't be able to feel it on the outside, his hand cradling mine just feels right.

"Hey there, sweet girl," he whispers.

"This is perfect," I sigh, clutching Cade's bicep as I glance up at him. He strokes my cheek and brings my lips to his for a soul stealing kiss.

"You're perfect," he murmurs.

I could've stayed there all night, in the stillness, watching the lights dance overhead, but it's getting chilly, so we head back to the warmth of the cabin. Cade pulls me through the front door, stopping in the kitchen. He snags a pen from the junk drawer and snatches my list off the fridge. I watch with a bemused expression as he adds one last item to my bucket list and promptly checks it off.

"There. Everything is as it should be."

SNOW MUCH FUN

Paige's Holiday Bucket List

O stars, do not recommend

- ⊗ Sledding (call archie)
- ✓ Visit tree farm
- ✓ Snowball fight
- ✓ Hot Cocoa
- ✓ Snow angels
- ✓ Secret santa
- ✓ Build a snowman
- ✓ Mistletoe kisses ← ★ 10/10 recommend
- ✓ Gingerbread redemption   xoxo Mags
- ✓ Kiss under the northern lights

Pizzelles!!

Epilogue - Mags

♫ *Kid on Christmas - Pentatonix ft. Meghan Trainor*

What was supposed to be a lonely Christmas in Toronto has turned into one of the best holidays in recent memory. Paige has been begging me to move down to Oak Ridge after graduation, but I'm feeling restless and my wandering soul is afraid to put down roots. But if anything could convince me to stay, it might just be more vacations like this one.

Cade hands Paige a small velvet box, kissing her on the cheek. As she opens it, her face lights up with pure joy. "It's beautiful," she says, holding up the gold chain with a ruby pendant on it. "Her birthstone? What if she comes early?"

"Then I'll just get you a new one," he says matter-of-factly. She sits on the floor between his thighs, allowing him to secure the necklace as she holds up her hair. His hands skate along her shoulders and he kisses her temple before she reaches out, plucking a delicately wrapped package off the coffee table.

Paige passes him his gift, and he wastes no time tearing open the wrapping. Pulling out a velvet wrapped book, he flips to the first page and his jaw drops. I watch in amusement as he turns to the next page. I already know about the boudoir photo album since I helped her put it together. Cade is practically drooling as he flips through the book, his eyes like saucers when he gets to the last page. "You still have this little outfit, Sunshine?"

"Mmmhmm," she says, her tone dripping with sensuality. And suddenly, I feel like I'm intruding on a very private moment.

"Hey guys, still here," I snort.

Cade leans down to kiss his wife before giving me an apologetic look. I love how much he loves my best friend, but damn, do I get jealous sometimes. I need a man who looks at me like I'm the last bite of chocolate cake. As they pull apart, Paige's phone lights up on the coffee table.

"Holy shit," she says. Turning the phone so I can read the text.

> Luca: Merry Christmas, baby sister. How would you feel about a new neighbor down in Oak Ridge?

Paige stares at her phone for several heartbeats as we all sit in stunned silence. Paige's relationship with her brother is complicated, but they've been working on a path to forgiveness for several months, and they're closer than they've ever been. She quickly taps out a reply.

> Paige: I think you've lost the plot, big bro. Are you moving?

> Luca: Thinking about it. Can you give me the number of that contractor Cade is friends with?

> Paige: Miles? Sure.

She sends off the link to his contact, and taps out one last text for good measure.

> Paige: Merry Christmas, Luca. And just in case it wasn't clear, I'd love to have you here.

"Does that mean what I think it means?" I ask.

She shrugs. "I guess he's thinking about moving here. I just wonder what gave him the push. I wouldn't be surprised if he had some kind of falling out with my parents."

After several minutes of quiet contemplation, Cade walks over to the tree, bending down to pick up something near the back. I frown in confusion when he comes back and stops directly in front of me. "This one's for you," he says, handing me a rather large, heavy box with a giant red bow but no tag. I tear into the gift wrap, brow furrowed as I consider what it could possibly contain.

My breath whooshes out of my lungs when I find a sage green vintage typewriter, already loaded with a paper that says "Merry Christmas." It must have cost a pretty penny to find one that's still in working condition with all the letters intact. Tears immediately spring to my eyes at the sight of the best gift

I've ever received. "Paige," her name comes out on a choked sob. "You shouldn't have."

She bites her bottom lip. "I wish I could take credit, but it wasn't me," she says.

"Then who?"

She just shrugs. "Secret Santa, I guess. Or, maybe the Grinch."

PART TWO

I'll be home for
CHRISTMAS

Archie and Rosie's Playlist

There are song titles accompanying every chapter.

Chapter 15

Archie

♫ *I'll Be Home for Christmas - Doris Day*

Winter, 1979
"Archie Sullivan! You get your muddy behind back outside before I call your daddy in here."

"Sorry, Ma." I chuckle at the all too familiar threat, the screen door slamming against the frame as I step back out into the frigid winter air. I tap my boots on the concrete porch steps leading up to a modest farmhouse on the outskirts of Oak Ridge, Kentucky. The once pristine dark green shutters are hanging loose, and the railing is wobbling — nothing a little elbow grease can't fix, but I'm bone tired after a long day working at the hardware store. I promised Mama we'd string up the garland and the lights this weekend, so maybe I can find some time for some repairs while I'm at it. Toeing off my boots on the welcome mat, I step back into the comfort of home, the smell of Mama's famous pot roast wafting through the air as the dull hum of Christmas music plays over the radio.

"Smells good, Ma," I say, kissing her on the cheek as she stands at the kitchen sink, rinsing off the dishes in her red polka dot apron.

She recoils slightly. "You smell like a wet dog. Go get cleaned up. The new neighbors are coming over for dinner tonight."

"New neighbors? They finally sell the old Beaumont place?" The rundown house next door has been in shambles for years, abandoned by the Beaumonts about 10 years back. Despite all the memories it holds, I'd considered buying it for myself as a pet project as soon as I saved up enough cash to get outta my childhood home. Because really, what self-respecting 27-year-old man is still living at home with his parents? Looks like that ship has sailed.

"Sure did. Nice older couple. Got a niece about your age," she replies, her expression telling me everything I need to know about this so-called friendly neighborhood welcome party. I'm walking straight into a trap and there's nothing I can do about it.

"I've told you a million times, I'm not lookin' to get shacked up with some outta towner who's not gonna stick around once she realizes there's nothin' but an old bookstore and a rundown bar across town for entertainment."

"It's a good thing I'm not some outta towner then, Archie Sullivan." The voice is familiar, haunting even. A callback to what feels like a past life. I close my eyes, not daring to turn around for fear that I've imagined her.

Rosie Beaumont.

My high school sweetheart.

The one that got away.

"Rosie Dear! D'you mind helping Archie here set the table?"

"No ma'am. Just point me to the silverware." Her lavender scent fills the air as footsteps sound nearby. I'm rooted to the spot, as if frozen in time — a time when I was head over boots in love with the girl next door. But she disappeared not long after homecoming without so much as a goodbye.

Chapter 16

Rosie

♫ *Have Yourself A Merry Little Christmas - Judy Garland*

Fall, 1969

"Get moving, Rosie girl. We have to be at the station in 45 minutes."

"I told you, Mama. I'm not goin'. I'll find a job, get an apartment. I'm not leaving Oak Ridge."

Mama's stands in the doorway of my now empty bedroom, face pained as she takes in my tear-stained cheeks. My entire life is packed up in one small suitcase, everything else sold off piece by piece just to afford the train tickets to Georgia. Last week, Daddy left us high and dry, taking everything with him, including Mama's heart, and what was left of our meager savings. We had no idea he was in so much trouble until he ran, leaving us to clean up his mess.

Mama contacted her sister in Georgia the next day, pleading for them to take us in. Aunt Bea didn't hesitate, making up our rooms, and sending enough money for us to get by for the week.

"I'm sorry, darlin'. You know we have no choice. Your daddy left us a helluva mess, and we can't stay here any longer."

Another piece of my heart breaks, hopelessness settling in my bones as I stare down at the worn carpet, still stained with pink nail polish from homecoming. "Can I stop at the Sullivan's before we go?" I ask, my voice barely above a whisper.

Mama's brows draw together as she gathers my hands in hers. "We don't have time. I'm sorry."

I'd tried to call Archie all day with no answer. He's probably out working the ranch, seeing as it's a Saturday. Between his part-time job working for his daddy at the hardware store, and his Saturdays at Whispering Oaks, his weekends are not his own.

Devastation consumes me as I pick up my suitcases and follow my mother out the front door. As we reach the end of the drive where I learned to ride a bike, I turn back to look at the only home I've ever known; to the yard where Beau is buried; to the porch steps where I stood when Archie Sullivan kissed me for the first time and the last time. "I'll come back for you," I whisper to no one in particular. "I promise."

Winter, 1979

He hasn't looked at me. Hasn't so much as turned around since I walked into the room, and I don't know how to feel about that. Does he remember me? Did he even miss me? Maybe he's moved on.

"Aunt Bea and Uncle Chuck wanted me to thank you for the invitation, but they're a little under the weather. It's just me for tonight."

"We're glad to have you, sweet girl. Now, if my son would get his head out of his behind, he'd realize he's standing right in front of the silverware drawer," Eleanor says, hip checking her son.

As Archie turns, I suck in a sharp breath. He's not the same boy he was when I left — it would be foolish of me to expect him to be. But the man standing before me is almost unrecognizable. His dark brown hair is tousled, a curl falling over his forehead that I wish I could reach out and touch. There's a neatly trimmed beard where I once caressed a bare cheek, but those eyes — those eyes are still the same. Bright blue depths that I could drown in over and over.

"Rosie."

My name on his lips is all I've wanted to hear for the better part of a decade. And after everything I've been through in my time away, what's left of my heart falls at his feet, begging him to pick it up and hold it in his hands as he once did.

He steps into my space, his muscular form blurry behind the tears that have built up along my lashes. "Hey now. What's wrong, darlin'?" I fall into his arms, sinking into the familiar warmth of the only boy I ever loved. He stiffens for only a moment before wrapping me in a soothing embrace.

"I'm sorry. I probably stink to high heaven," he chuckles. "I didn't get a chance to get cleaned up." He doesn't. There's an earthy scent — no doubt from working outside — but underneath that is something musky and comforting — like home. "Come sit with me?" he asks, a hint of hesitation in his voice. Words escape me, so I nod.

Chapter 17

Archie

♫ *All Alone on Christmas - Darlene Love*

I can't believe she's here. It feels like a dream and yet I can see her, hear her, touch her. She has pulled up her golden hair with a red ribbon, and her blue eyes still sparkle despite the tears trailing down her cheeks. She still barely reaches my chin, but her figure is fuller and fuck if she doesn't look every bit as good as I imagined she would. My Rosie girl, all grown up. Despite what she might think of me, I never forgot my first love — my only love.

Despite my reputation around town, there's never been anyone I considered being with long-term. Rosie is — was — it for me. Over the years I'd had one offs to keep me satisfied, but my heart only ever belonged to one woman. Seeing her again is like a jolt to my system — heady and unfamiliar.

I take her by the hand, leading her through the house to the living room, where I guide her down onto the yellow sofa. Angling my body to face hers, I take her hands in mine. "Tell me."

She doesn't have to ask what I mean. She knows. The last time I saw Rosie Beaumont, she was stepping onto a train with a suitcase and a handkerchief. Her long blonde hair pulled back in a scarf with a blank look on her face. She never called, and I never saw her again.

"I don't know where to start," she says, staring off at Mama's Christmas tree in the corner of the room. The faint sound of dishes clanking in the kitchen is the only sound as I wait on bated breath for Rosie to tell me her story. To finally get the answers I've waited so long to hear.

On instinct, I give her hand a reassuring squeeze — a gesture so familiar yet foreign. Despite my urge to hold her, I don't know Rosie Beaumont anymore, and she's not mine. "How 'bout we start with where you've been for the last 10 years, and go from there?"

She exhales a breath, her eyes locking with mine for a beat before she speaks. "About a week before I left, Daddy ran off with all of our money and damn near everything we owned. He'd been in debt for months, and somebody was after him. Mama said we couldn't stay, so we packed up and moved to Georgia to live with Aunt Bea. I tried to tell you, but I couldn't find you that day."

My heart sinks at how lost she must have felt. I would've gone to her had I known. "I was at the station, Rosie. I saw you."

"What do you mean?" She eyes be curiously, waiting for my answer.

"We were meeting up with Uncle Tommy. You were on the other side of the platform, stepping onto the train and fuck, Ro, I wanted to run to you so badly. I didn't know I was never gonna see you again or I would have." Deep down I'd known something was wrong, but I fought against my instincts, telling myself I'd see her at school on Monday.

"I wrote to you, but they always came back to me. Aunt

Bea didn't have a phone line, so I called every day for a week from a pay phone in town. Eventually, I ran out of what little money I had and I gave up. But I never forgot, Arch. Not for a single day. And then —" I can tell she wants to say more, but she stops herself. I want to pry, but this is her story to tell, and if she's not ready, I can't force it. I just have to be here when she is ready.

Her eyes are haunted, leaving me to wonder what her life has been like for the last 10 years. I know mine has felt empty. Like I'm going through the motions but not really livin'. Having Rosie here, in my space — it was shifting something in me, and I knew without a shadow of a doubt I wasn't gonna let her get away again.

"Why are you back?" I ask, only now realizing my Mama mentioned an older couple with a niece — fuck. She knew. She fucking knew, and she didn't tell me it was Rosie.

"Mama got sick." Her tears start flowing again and my heart breaks for the woman in front of me. A woman who, for all I know, is little more than a stranger now, but feels so familiar to me. "She died last year and I couldn't stay in that house anymore. Too many memories."

Unable to hold myself back any longer, I pull her into my arms, wishing I could take the grief from her. "I'm sorry, darlin'." Rosie's mother was a kind woman, if a little meek. She taught Rosie how to bake, and welcomed me with open arms where other mothers might've been wary of their daughters spending so much time with the boy next door.

She pulls away, sniffling and swiping away the tears. "So how've you been, Arch?" The way she so casually shifts from inconsolable to casual has my hackles up. Who taught her to hide her emotions behind all that fake brightness? And how do I fix what they've broken?

"Not much has changed for me, I'm afraid. Took over the

store from Pops last year. He was badly injured in an accident and can't get around like he used to." Her delicate hand reaches out to squeeze my forearm, and I place my hand over hers, keeping her trapped there. The touch is soothing in a way I haven't felt in years; in a way only she has ever affected me. "He still comes in most days, but he works the register and chats with the regulars. All the hard labor falls to me. I keep up the house and help mama 'round here as much as she'll let me"

"Seems like life ain't been too kind to either of us," she says, her eyes trained on where our bodies are connected before she pulls away. "It's good to see you, Archie."

I nod, unable to come up with a response. I want to ask her if she's seeing someone, if she's fallen in love and had children and lived the life she's always dreamed of. Does she still like to cook? Did she open the diner like she'd always dreamed? Did she get another dog after Beau? I have so many questions and yet I can't seem to voice them.

"Well, if it isn't little Rosie Beaumont," Dad drawls, leaning heavily on his cane as he joins us in the living room. "You're all grown up." He opens one arm for a hug and Rosie indulges him, squeezing my dad tightly for a moment.

"Good to see you, Sully," she says.

"You, too. Darlin'. You sure are a sight for sore eyes." Pops has always been a charmer — I get a little of that from him, I guess. And he always loved little Rosie Beaumont like one of his own. I'm an only child, though it wasn't for lack of trying. For years, Rosie filled an empty space in their hearts. They were just as devastated as I was when she left. If even one of those letters had made it here, I know Mama would've found a way to bring them back home to Oak Ridge. "Y'all should get back to the kitchen and set that table 'fore Mama comes in here swinging that rolling pin."

I chuckle, pulling Rosie along behind me towards the kitchen where Mama's standing with her arms crossed, rolling pin in hand, trying to hide her smirk. She's up to somethin' and I think I know just what that is. Normally, I'd try to get away from her schemes, but if she wants me woo-ing Rosie Beaumont, I won't fight that one bit.

Chapter 18

Rosie

♫ *White Christmas - Bing Crosby*

"That's enough tinsel, my love."

"But Mama, it's so pretty!" I pluck a strand from my little girl's blonde hair, watching the wonder on her face as she covers another branch with the glittery threads.

"Listen to your mother, Lottie girl," Aunt Bea says, patting my 7-year-old on the head. She turns to face me next, a knowing look on her face. "How was dinner with the Sullivans?"

Aunt Bea knows all about Archie — she spent many a night holding me while I cried over the boy I thought I'd never see again. Charlotte's dad came along somewhere in my haze of loss and grief, with pretty promises that turned out to be snake oil. He was older than me, and as soon as I found out I was pregnant at 18, fresh out of high school, he left without a word. Turns out he had a whole family of his own in the city, and I'd been nothing more than a pretty little distraction.

Lottie's been my whole world ever since, and as much as I

want to fall right back into things with Archie, I'm not sure how we fit together anymore. We've grown up, and Lottie is my priority; being with me means being with her — we're a package deal, and for some men that would be a tough pill to swallow.

When I ran into Mrs. Sullivan at the market, Lottie was with Aunt Bea, so she doesn't know I have a daughter, and I didn't bring it up. In a panic, I thought up a story about my aunt and uncle being sick so I wouldn't have to tell them about the invitation. It's better this way.

I need to figure out how I'm going to tell Archie; though it's presumptuous of me to think he even wants anything to do with me after so long. But his hands on my skin felt so familiar. And the way he held me — I could cry just thinking about it.

The doorbell chimes, startling me out of my thoughts. "I'll get that," Aunt Bea says, striding towards the front door. "Hi there. Can I help you?"

A familiar voice responds, sending shivers coursing through me. "I'm Archie Sullivan, ma'am. I'm here to see Rosie."

"Of course. It's nice to finally meet you. Come right on in." As soon as the invitation is out of her mouth, I freeze. He's about to walk in here any second and come face to face with my girl. Ready or not, Rosie girl.

I walk over to Lottie, crouching down to her level. "Sweetie, there's someone I want you to meet. He's a nice man. An old friend of mine from when I was younger." In true Lottie fashion, she crinkles her nose at me in confusion, then returns to her task, completely unfazed.

I stand a little taller, swiping my hands over my skirt just as Aunt Bea follows Archie into the room. It's a modest space; a little more weathered than it was the last time I was here, but we've been fixing it up as we unpack. The Christmas decorations provide a more inviting atmosphere than we'd have otherwise, distracting from the chipped paint and peeling wallpaper.

"Mornin' Ro. Mama sent me over with some fresh baked muffins," Archie says, his voice trailing off when his gaze snags on the little girl with the tinsel strewn everywhere.

I quickly step into his space, reaching for the basket of muffins. "Tell your mama thank you for me. This is really thoughtful. Do you want to sit for a spell?"

He nods, eyeing me warily before taking a seat on the plush green sofa. Placing the basket on the table, I take a seat at the far end, keeping my distance in case this conversation doesn't end well. "Aunt Bea, can you take Lottie to the kitchen? Let her try one of Elanor's muffins while me and Archie catch up."

She nods, holding out a hand for my little girl, who skips out to the hallway with a smile on her face and a basket of muffins in hand. Motherhood is strange — like walking around with your heart outside of your body. I wasn't prepared for it the way I wish I had been, but we got by, and I love that girl down to my bones.

"Is she —"

I cut him off before he can finish his question. "Mine? Yes."

"She looks just like you," he says, inching a little closer to me on the sofa. "How old is she?"

"She's 7. Her name is Charlotte, but we call her Lottie."

"And her daddy?"

"Not in the picture." I glance down at my hands, fidgeting with a wayward stitch on my skirt. "We didn't plan it. And he didn't want kids. Or me, as it turns out."

Archie's hand covers mine. When I look up, he's gazing at me attentively, and I wonder what he sees there. Can he see the broken woman? Can he see the girl I once was underneath?

"Forgive me if I'm oversteppin'. Can I meet her?"

I smile then, a spark of hope blooming in the middle of my chest. "Yes. I'd like that. But if we peel her away from the muffins, I think there'll be hell to pay. Let me take you to the kitchen." Archie chuckles at that, and the deep sound reverberates through the room, sending shivers down my spine.

"Just like her mama, huh? You always did like to squirrel away a few of those muffins for yourself. Lead the way."

Archie

She has a daughter. And, my god, she's the spitting image of Rosie. At first, I was hurt — too focused on the grief of losing her all over again and the life I thought we'd share. But then I saw the nervous way she picked at her skirt, and the sadness in her eyes, and I knew. In the very depths of my soul, I knew this was my second chance. Someone hurt this girl — deeply — and I'll do everything in my power to fix it.

"Lottie, I'd like to you meet Mr. Sullivan," she says, speaking to the little blonde-haired girl with the muffin crumbs tumbling out of her mouth. "Oh my. Get a napkin, honey. You're a mess." Her face lights up as she speaks to her daughter, washing away any sign of the pain she hides beneath the surface.

"Call me Archie, darlin'. Mr. Sullivan makes me sound old."

She swallows the last of her muffin, smiling sweetly, but there's a hint of mischief in her eyes. "You are old. Like my mama, right? She said you're an old friend."

"Ouch, Lottie. That hurt," I tease. "I'd like to be your friend, too, if that's alright. It's very nice to meet you."

She shrugs in response, each gesture reminding me of a version of Rosie I thought was long gone. "Okay."

As far as introductions go, this was far less dramatic than I expected, and I'm not sure where to go from here, so I search Rosie's face for a clue. "She's pretty easygoing," she says. "I don't think she's ever met a stranger. A blessing and a curse, truly."

"Can I..." I swipe a hand through the haphazard mop that I call hair. "Can I take you for lunch? Both of you?"

"You want to have lunch with us?" Her voice is small, almost delicate, as she scans my face for something — though I'm not sure what. It makes me wonder what kind of shit she's dealt with in her past that she would doubt my sincerity.

"Yeah, Ro. It's been 10 years. I want to get to know you, and that includes Lottie — she's a part of you, too." I place my hands on her shoulders, waiting for her response. Her bottom lip quivers as she blinks rapidly.

When she finally responds, her voice is barely above a whisper. "I'd like that very much."

Chapter 19

Rosie

♫ *Blue Christmas - Elvis Presley*

Archie pulls up in his same old dark blue pickup, though it's more worn than it had been the last time I'd ridden in it. He helps Lottie into the middle of the bench seat, securing her seatbelt as I hoist myself up into the truck. Once we're secure, he closes my door and takes his seat behind the wheel.

"You ladies up for an adventure?" he asks, his devastatingly handsome smile on full display beneath his beard.

"What'd you have in mind?" I ask.

He extends his arm along the back of the seats, absent-mindedly playing with my blonde hair that I'd spent way too long perfecting in the mirror. Farrah Fawcett I'm not, but I think it turned out ok, all the same. "Not much has changed in this town since you left. We still don't have a decent restaurant, so I was thinkin' I'd take y'all to a little dive in Willow Valley."

Excited at the prospect of an adventure, Lottie bounces in

her seat. "I guess she approves. Lead the way, honey." The term of endearment slips out as if no time has passed. His lips curve into a smile as my cheeks heat and I avert my gaze, not wanting him to see me blush.

Christmas carols play over the radio as Archie navigates the familiar streets of Oak Ridge, and it feels as though I've gone back in time. Holiday decorations adorn the shops, with wreaths on every door and window along Main Street, except for a boarded up shop right in the middle. "Didn't that used to be Anita's Bakery?"

Archie follows my line of sight to the dilapidated building as we roll to a stop. "Went out of business a few years back. From what I've heard, Anita fell on hard times and moved in with her kids and grandkids for a spell."

"That's a shame. She always had the best pies."

"Didn't hold a candle to yours, Rosie girl."

"Mama makes the best pecan pie!" Lottie adds. "And cherry!" She smacks her lips as though tasting the confection right here in the truck.

"I was always pretty partial to the pumpkin pie, myself," he says, winking at my daughter.

The rest of the drive passes in companionable silence, the dull hum of the radio the only sound filling the cab. "We're here," he says, pulling up alongside an adorable diner in the heart of Willow Valley. Its exterior is vintage with silver accents and red lettering. The interior is much the same, but with a checkerboard floor and a long countertop with round stools. There's a large Christmas tree taking up part of the entryway, with garlands and string lights beyond. It's gaudy in the most adorable way. There's a large jukebox in the corner playing Blue Christmas, and the smell of fresh fries assaults my senses, causing my stomach to grumble loudly. "Let's get you fed before you wither away on me."

The server saunters over with a Santa hat and a little extra sparkle in her eye as she catches sight of Archie, and I'm immediately on alert. "Well hey there, handsome. Your usual?"

"Hey Denise. Actually, can we get a few menus?"

She glances over at me; her smile faltering slightly before her gaze moves to my daughter. "You got it," she says coldly.

"Friend of yours?" I ask, a hint of annoyance in my voice.

Archie turns on his stool, caging me between his muscular thighs. "Ancient history, Ro."

"More ancient than our 10 years?" I deadpan.

"That's different, darlin'. You were...are... fuck. I don't know how to do this anymore." He rakes a hand through his hair, a nervous gesture from his teen years that's so familiar it sends a pang of longing straight through my heart.

"It's okay, Archie. I know you have a past. I shouldn't have —" my words trail off as I consider what to say next. "I... I was jealous," I admit.

He smirks then, his eyes lighting up at my confession. "Nothin' to be jealous of," he says. Then his gaze softens with a tenderness I haven't seen in years. "It's only ever been you."

His words hit me like a bolt of lightning to my heart. He couldn't possibly mean that. There had to have been someone in the last 10 years. Hell, I went and had a whole life — a baby. But his face shows no sign of deception and I wonder what kind of life he's been living — has he been lonely? I wish I could ask him. But with Lottie here, I have to tread lightly.

When Denise returns with our menus, Archie tells us all about his favorite items, and Lottie's eyes snag on a giant stack of pancakes in the all day breakfast category. I decide on a classic grilled cheese and fries, and Arch orders the same along with a chocolate milkshake — my favorite. "Can we get two straws, Dee? Thanks."

I don't miss the way she rolls her eyes as she runs back to the kitchen, and by now I find her indignation amusing. Let her be jealous of me. I don't think I've ever had something worth being jealous of until now. If I even *have* Archie, that is. *He certainly has me.*

Archie

I don't know what's more delicious, the grilled cheese or the sight of Rosie's lips around the straw, sucking up the thick chocolate milkshake I knew she'd love. Makes me wanna see her lips wrapped around somethin' else. Ever since she stepped into my truck in those skintight jeans, I've been hard as a fucking rock. Time has only made her more beautiful.

Lottie's eyes were bigger than her appetite, that's for sure. She's halfway through the stack of pancakes and her eyes are at half mast. "You okay there, darlin'?"

"Mmmhmm," she mumbles.

Rosie checks the time on the large clock above the counter. "You tired, sweetheart?" Lottie nods, leaning her head against Rosie's shoulder. "She's had trouble adjusting to her new surroundings, so she hasn't been sleeping well. I oughta get her home to bed."

I pay the check, leaving a decent tip for Denise despite the clear disdain she showed my companions. "Let's get you girls home," I say. Lottie's hand reaches for mine, her small palm engulfed by my much larger one, and the gesture damn near knocks me on my ass. She reaches for her mama with the other hand, and I'm certain we make a pretty picture; the perfect little family. Fuck, I want this so badly. But I can't push it. I know she's been through a lot and she's not just gonna instantly accept me back into her life and trust me with her daughter. I have a long way to go before we get to "happy family", but fuck if I'm not gonna give it everthin' I've got. The second she walked back into my life, I'd claimed her. She just didn't know it yet.

When I pull up to the familiar white farmhouse next door

to my childhood home, I take note of the crooked spindles on the railing and the chipped paint on the door frame. All things considered, they've done a good job of cleaning up the place. But I can tell it needs some work.

Lottie's soft snores fill the silence as I put the truck in park. Before Rosie can pull her out of her seat, I'm lifting her into my arms and settling her against my chest.

"You don't have to do that," Rosie says, reaching out to take her from me. But before she can, I spot Aunt Bea sauntering down the steps. "You give that girl to me and get on outta here," she says. "I'm on babysitting duty. You two go have some alone time. Lord knows you need it." She winks at Rosie, taking a peaceful Lottie up the steps and through the front door.

"We don't have to —"

I take a step forward, caging her against my truck. "You don't really think I'm gonna let you get away that easily, do ya? Your Aunt just gave me a whole afternoon and I'm gonna make the most of it, Rosie girl. You ready?"

Her eyes flick to my lips, and as much as I've been dying to kiss her, I force myself to pull away. I want her to be sure of some things before we go there. Because once I've kissed her again, she's mine and I'm never letting go. "Get in the truck, darlin'."

Chapter 20

Archie

♫ *Sleigh Ride - The Carpenters*

Summer, 1968
Rosie and Archie, Age 16

"I'm so sorry, Ro. Beau was such a good dog."

She sniffles, her tears soaking my shirt, fists clinging to the fabric as we sit side by side on her front porch. "I'm gonna miss him so much." She inhales stuttered breaths between words and it breaks my heart to see her hurting like this. Is this what love feels like? Wanting to take all the pain and keep it for myself so she never has to feel it? Wanting to kiss it all away so she never has to cry another tear? I think it might be something close.

I stroke a hand along her golden locks, bringing my nose to her hair to inhale her flowery scent. "Let's go to the lake," I whisper. *Beau wouldn't want you to be sad. We can swim for a*

125

while. He would've loved that. Remember how he used to paddle around in the shallows?"

She glances up at me through her wet lashes, a faint smile ghosting across her face. Instinctively, my hand cups her cheek. Wanting to keep that smile for myself, I tilt her chin to bring us eye to eye. Her pulse thrums beneath my fingertips as her eyes dart to my lips, and I wonder if this is the moment. But it feels wrong. She's crying and I don't want to take advantage when she's vulnerable. Our first kiss should be special. Not like this.

My swirling thoughts are interrupted as Rosie presses her soft lips against mine in a whisper of a kiss. She pulls back before I can respond and our eyes lock. The moment lingers for seconds, minutes maybe. Then, ever so slowly, I bring my mouth back to hers, giving her every opportunity to stop me. But she doesn't. Instead, she leans into my touch and steals the air from my lungs when her tongue sweeps along my bottom lip. I open for her, deepening the kiss. Nothing else matters in that moment but the feel of her skin beneath my palm, and the taste of her on my lips. If this isn't love, I don't know what is.

Chapter 21

Rosie

♫ *(There's No Place Like) For the Holidays - Perry Como*

Winter, 1979

My brow furrows as Archie pulls the truck into the drive just one house down from mine.

"My parents are visiting my uncle for the weekend. We have the house to ourselves," he explains. "Thought maybe we could spend some time together? Catch up?" His hesitancy is endearing the sweetest way. That he wants to make sure I'm comfortable means more to me than I think he realizes.

"I'd love that, Arch." I lean over and peck his cheek before stepping out of the truck. The cool bite of winter air hits my face as I pull my coat tighter around me.

"C'mon. I'll make some cocoa and light the fire to keep us warm."

It sounds like heaven. "You had me at cocoa."

"You had me long before that. But I'll give you some time to catch up," he says, so nonchalantly that it catches me off guard. I stop dead in my tracks, stunned silent as I replay the words over and over until they sound so foreign that I snort out a laugh. "You laughin' at me, Ro?"

"Yeah. I think I am," I say, blinking back tears of laughter. "You've gone soft, Archie Sullivan."

He quirks a brow in my direction and my cheeks heat as I glance down at the visible bulge in his jeans. *Ok, so maybe not so soft.*

With a steaming mug of cocoa in hand, and a view of Archie's round ass as he stokes the fire, I slip into what feels like pure bliss. If I stay here long enough, maybe the questions and worries that await me will all disappear. I don't have a job; I have to enroll Lottie in school, and I still don't have a long-term plan for the future. Are we staying here for good? Is that even an option? There are so many questions left unanswered, but right now, in the quiet of Archie's childhood home, with only the warmth from fire in the hearth and the sound of crackling embers filling the silence, it feels as though maybe those things don't matter so much.

The cushion dips as Archie sinks down beside me. "Ro?"

"Huh?"

"I asked if you're okay. You looked a little far away for a minute."

"Just thinkin'. Do you remember the Christmas that Mama E made us decorate our own ornaments?"

"How could I forget? You used so much glitter we could probably still find some in the carpet if we look close enough."

"You were the one that made me spill it!" I scold, my smile faltering slightly as I recall more of the memory. "You wrote Rosie Sullivan on the back of mine."

His eyes crinkle at the corners when he smiles. "I did." He takes a sip of his cocoa, as though what I just said wasn't the most monumental moment of our entire relationship. Until that point, we had been best friends. My 15-year-old heart landed in the palm of his hand that day and he didn't even know it. Silence stretches between us, the memory lingering in the air like a ghost.

"Thing is, I have a million memories just like that one," he says, setting his holiday mug down on the table in front of us as he turns his body to face me. "You could ask me to list off every one of my best childhood memories and you'd be there in every single one of 'em. You were always there, Ro. Until you weren't."

"I'm s —"

His finger presses against my lips, cutting off my apology. "Don't apologize, darlin'. Not your fault. But damn, is it good to see you again. Let's not dwell on the past, alright? Not when you're right here in front of me."

I try not to let on just how much his words affect me. "There you go again, you big 'ol softie."

We spend the rest of the afternoon sharing 10 years' worth of memories. I lay everything bare, from the moment I found out I was pregnant, to Mama's last words as she slipped away from me. I don't cry. Truth is, I don't think I have any tears left in me. But Archie listens to every word, asking questions to fill the silence. And when I run out of things to say, he tells me about his life. About his dad's car accident and taking over the shop, the almost monthly dates his mom tries to set him up on, and how he takes care of them both, making sure they have everything they need and then some. By the end of it all, I'm certain of one thing — Archie Sullivan is a good man.

Willa Kay

Quite possibly the best man I've ever known, and I'm in way over my head.

Chapter 22

Rosie

♫*Walking in a Winter Wonderland - Michael Bublé*

It's been a week since dinner at the Sullivan's, and I've seen Archie every day since. We've slipped into an easy routine, sharing meals and swapping stories. He drops off breakfast every morning, saying a quick hello to Lottie before heading in to work. We've settled back into a comfortable friendship — nothing more. But with every moment he's around, I crave more. Can I afford to lose my heart again if this life we're building here isn't permanent? There are still too many unanswered questions.

Archie parks his truck along Main Street, the quiet hum of the engine coming to a stop outside of the bookshop. Ever the gentleman, he helps me out of the passenger seat and a shiver courses through me, not from the chill in the air, but from the touch of his hand as his fingers thread between mine. "This alright?" he asks, his gaze flicking down to our now joined hands.

I nod. "Where are we going?"

"Nowhere in particular," he says, tugging me onto the sidewalk. "Thought we could take a walk."

As we stroll down the once familiar streets of Oak Ridge, it's like I'm transported back in time. I haven't had a chance to explore much since coming back to town, but everything seems relatively unchanged. It's both comforting and unsettling.

The shops are all decorated for Christmas, with twinkle lights and wreaths adorning each one. There are signs for a Christmas tree decorating contest in the windows, asking patrons to vote on their favorite — each one more extravagant than the last. I stop in front of the flower shop, admiring its pastel pink tree decorated in what must be hundreds of blooms. It's breathtakingly beautiful and I can't help but stare. Archie tugs on my arm, pushing through the doorway into the shop, the bell chiming overhead, signaling our arrival.

"Betty, can we get one of those contest ballots?"

A stout woman in her 50s approaches the counter with a small white slip of paper in hand. She looks familiar but I can't quite place her. "Well hey there, Archie. Is that — Rosie Beaumont, as I live and breathe! I heard you were back in town, but I didn't believe it. It's good to see you, dear."

"Mrs. Thompson? My goodness, I almost didn't recognize you." My high school history teachers pull me in for a hug, damn near squeezing the life outta me.

"Bet you've got this one wrapped around your finger again, huh?" She points towards Archie with a chuckle. I follow the gesture in time to see his wide smile as he shrugs.

"Never could resist 'er. We just came in to vote for your tree. Thought Rosie was gonna faint when she saw it."

Mrs. Thompson blushes at his praise, handing over the slip of paper and a pen.

"It is beautiful," I say with a smile as I jot down my vote

before dropping it into the ballot box on the counter. "It was good to see you, Mrs. Thompson."

"You can call me Betty, dear. I'm not your teacher anymore. Good to have you back. Careful with this one, he'll steal your heart if you're not careful."

Might be too late, Betty.

On our way out of the flower shop, Archie stops abruptly. "Stay here. I'll be right back."

With a nod, I step out onto the sidewalk, inhaling the fresh winder air. It smells like we're gonna get snow. I know that sounds insane; Kentucky isn't exactly known for its winter weather. But there's a crispness to the air right before snowfall — it smells more earthy and fresh somehow. The bell above the flower shop chimes again as Archie steps out onto the curb with a bouquet of red roses and carnations surrounded by evergreen sprigs. "For you, m'lady."

I giggle as he hands me the bouquet that looks like Christmas and feels like more. "Did you just m'lady me like some knight of the round table?"

"Depends. Did you like it?"

Before I can think better of it, the words tumble out of my mouth unbidden. "I like you."

He reaches for my hand and kisses my knuckles. "I like you, too."

With my paper wrapped bundle of flowers in hand, Archie leads me further down the sideway, passing several locals who smile and nod at my companion. Most don't recognize me, and I can't really fault 'em for it. Several women balk in my direction before thinking better of it, and I wonder, not for the first time, how many of them he's been with.

When we pass by the boarded up bakery again, a distant ache settles deep in my bones. I stop for a moment, tugging my hand free to peek through the window. It looks just as I remember it, only barren and sad. The display cases that once held the most delicious pastries call to me like a beacon. The tables are still there, with chairs flipped upside down as though they intended to come back the next day but never did.

We continue walking for a spell before he pulls me to a stop at a park bench near Sully's Hardware, the cold bite of the wood seeping through my clothes as I take a seat. I gravitate closer to Archie on instinct and he smiles, wrapping an arm around my shoulder as we cling to each other for warmth. My nose prickles as the chill sets in.

"Tell me more about your life," he says, a look of genuine curiosity on his face.

"I can't think of anything we haven't covered already. What do you wanna know?"

He contemplates for a beat, as though he has a finite number of questions and he wants to ask the right ones to get the information he's looking for. His lips curve into a small smile when he seems to come to a conclusion. "Do you still love to cook?"

I sigh wistfully. "More than ever, I think. But Lottie's become very particular, so I don't get to be too adventurous with my recipes these days."

"You can test out new recipes on me any day. Did you ever get to open your restaurant down in Georgia?" The question hits me like a punch to the gut — that long-held dream all but forgotten when we left Kentucky. I clung to it for years, hoping I could make a go of it once I graduated, but all hope fled the moment Josh left me with a baby to care for and only my small, close-knit family for support.

Uncertain how to answer his question without laying myself bare before him, I decide to be straightforward. "No."

His fingers stroke over my knuckles, the tender gesture leaving me aching for more. "Is that something you'd like to do here?"

"Honestly? I haven't given it much thought. Lottie's my

world. Everything I do is for her. I figured I'd look for a job at one of the shops in town for now and see where that takes me."

"Great. You're hired," he says, his face practically beaming.

"What do you mean?"

"I need some help 'round the shop and you need a job. Seems pretty simple to me. I've been workin' myself to the bone these past weeks with the holidays coming up. You'd be doin' me a favor. Besides, I'd get to see your pretty face every day."

"Archie Sullivan, are you flirtin' with me?"

"Always, Rosie Beaumont. Always."

"You already get to see me every day when you drop off breakfast."

He smiles. "Well, now I'll be dropping off breakfast *and* picking you up for work."

Looking like the cat who got the cream, he tugs me to standing, wrapping an arm around my waist as we continue our walk down main street. "Now that's settled —"

"Hmmm. I don't recall saying yes."

"Didn't say no, neither. Just think about it. You don't have to give me an answer yet."

We stroll in companionable silence down the sidewalk, the shop signs switching from open to close as the sun sinks below the horizon, casting a warm glow over the town that feels more and more like home. Archie's arm leaves my waist, skating along my forearm to intertwine our now icy fingers. "Let's get back to the truck before you freeze to death. Can't have that now that I've finally got you back."

His words send butterflies dancing in my belly, but I tamp them down. I can't get too attached. My future is still so uncertain and I have Lottie to think about. Turning back the way we came, silence stretches between us, his gaze flicking to

135

mine every few steps as though he's waiting for me to say something, anything to ease the tension.

The truck comes into view just as a snowflake lands on my nose, stopping me in my tracks. A smile washes over my face as I tilt my head to the sky. "Archie, look." Another lands on my upturned palm, followed by another and another as the sky opens up; each one melting on my skin, leaving nothing but a tiny droplet of water. At the sound of my voice, he turns, something sweet passing over his features as he stares at me. One side of his mouth tips up as he pulls me into his arms, one palm landing on his chest.

"There's somethin' I wanna make clear to you, Rosie Beaumont." His warmth envelopes me as his nose brushes against mine, making my heart race. "I want you. More than my next breath. I've wanted you since before that first hello, and long after our last goodbye."

My breath hitches. "Oh."

"Yeah. Oh." He gently cups my cheek, the snow coming down around us, though nothing seems to matter but his presence. "Tell me you don't want this and I'll walk back to the truck. We'll drive straight home and I'll drop you off. We can forget this day ever happened."

"Or?"

"Or kiss me, Ro. Kiss me like you mean it."

And hell... what kind of choice is that? I lift onto my tiptoes, lightly brushing my nose against his as his arms tighten around my waist. When his soft lips meet mine, it's as if the world stops turning. Nothing exists in that moment but us. Not the snow, not the weight of our past, not even the uncertainty of the future.

As he deepens the kiss, I part my lips allowing him to taste me. His tongue dances with mine, and those butterflies are back in full force. My hand finds the nape of his neck, playing with the curls there as I nip playfully at his bottom lip. He smiles against my mouth, nipping back before pressing into me again. A growl erupts from his throat, sending a shiver down my spine. "Let's get in the truck, Rosie girl. 'Fore I take you right here on the sidewalk."

"Take me?"

"Claim you. Fuck you. Tell the whole damn world you're mine."

My eyes widen in shock as the words hang between us. "You —"

"Can't? Won't? Shouldn't?"

Against every instinct to flee, I laugh at his boldness. "All of the above?"

"Could, would, and should, darlin'. But you deserve better. I've waited a long time to have you again, and I'm not gonna do it on the sidewalk along Main Street, much as I'd like everyone to know Rosie Beaumont's my girl."

"Your girl, huh? Not sure I agreed to that, either."

"You will."

I will.

The air is thick with desire when Archie pulls away from the curb. Before I can think better of it, I boldly slip to the middle of the bench seat, my hand finding his thigh as though I can't stand to not be touching him. And I'm surprised to find I don't mind giving in to the pull. "Careful, Ro. You're playin' a dangerous game."

Absent-mindedly tugging my bottom lip between my teeth, I slide my hand higher over the very prominent bulge in his jeans. "What if I wanna play?" I squeeze around his rock hard length, eliciting a guttural groan from deep in his chest.

With the snow blanketing the once barren landscape, he rolls to a stop at the last intersection before our street. "You play with fire, you're gonna get burned."

I shift to face him, bringing both hands to his belt buckle. My lips graze his ear, his beard scraping against my cheek as I speak the words that are sure to be my undoing. "Burn me."

Chapter 23

Archie

♫ *Merry Christmas Baby - Bruce Springsteen*

B *urn me.*

Fuck me. I don't know where this newfound boldness came from, but I'm not gonna look a gift horse in the mouth, that's for sure. I pull onto a dirt road at the back of our property as Rosie pulls down my zipper, my hard cock straining against my boxers. Once we're a safe distance from the house, I tuck us behind a few of the larger trees, keeping us hidden from view. There's no way in hell I'm gonna let someone see my girl like this — vulnerable and sexy as hell. I've been craving her like this since the moment she walked into Mama's kitchen.

I lift my hips, allowing her to pull down my jeans. "Ro, baby. Slow down."

"I've had 10 years of slow, Archie. I need you." Before I can think twice, she's pulling her shirt over her head, giving me a gorgeous view of her lush body, every dip and curve on full display. Her nipples pebble behind black lace, and goose-flesh marks her skin. She wraps her fist around me, stroking slowly up and down my length as I unclasp her bra.

"What do you want, Rosie girl?" I pull her to me, my hand fisting in the back of her hair as my thumb traces the side of her jaw. "Tell me and I'll give it to you."

Her breathing picks up as her hand slows. "Everything." I crush my mouth to hers, groaning on contact as we taste each other like it's the first time. And I guess it is. For this version of us.

My hand slides along her ribs, cupping her full breast as she picks up the pace. I throw my head back, enjoying the feel of her skin on mine. My eyes are closed so I don't see her dip down, her tongue tracing the vein from root to tip. "Fuuuuuuck." I groan, looking down at my girl, who's staring at me through her lashes, a smile tugging at her lips. She takes me in her mouth, damn near sucking the life outta me. "You keep it up, this'll be over before it even starts."

At my warning, she straightens, working at the button on her jeans until she's completely bared to me, her neat tuft of curls visible below her soft belly. I glide two fingers through her wetness, circling her clit as she moans. Pulling away, I pat my lap. "Get up here, Ro. Wanna watch you ride me."

Without an ounce of hesitation, she straddles my lap. Her thick thighs clench around my hips as I line myself up with her center. She lowers herself inch by delicious inch, repeating the motion slowly as she adjusts to my size. "Good girl. You're taking me so well." She exhales a stuttered breath as she sinks down, taking me all the way to the hilt. "Fuck. I'm not gonna last long. You're strangling my cock. So tight. So perfect for me."

"You feel so good," she moans, rocking her hips back and forth as much as she can with the steering wheel digging into her back.

"Hold on." She wraps her arms around my neck as I shift us into the middle seat, giving her more space to move. "Take what you need, baby."

And she does. Rosie lifts onto her knees and sinks back down, over and over, setting an almost frantic pace, chasing her release. My hands grip her hips in a way that'll surely leave a mark, but I can't even be sorry about that. She's fucking perfect. I watch in awe as her hand reaches between us, circling her clit. I allow her this pleasure for only a moment before I'm gripping her wrist and pulling her fingers to my mouth for a taste. I moan around them. "All mine," I growl.

I replace her hand with my own, building her higher and higher until her pussy clenches around me, and I know she's close. "Be a good girl and come for me, Rosie." I don't know if it's my words that are her undoing, but she's certainly mine as she comes undone, her orgasm pulling me over the edge with her. As we come down from the high, I hold her to my chest. Her heartbeat falling in sync with mine, like two halves of the same whole.

"How is it I'm naked as a jaybird while you're still pretty much covered?" She asks, teasing the buttons on my shirt.

"I'm not complainin'," I quip. "Best damn view in town."

She giggles, and the sound pierces my heart. "Snow's really coming down now," she says, staring out the passenger window. "It's beautiful. Almost peaceful."

I push her hair over her shoulder, kissing the spot behind her ear that used to drive her wild. She shivers as my lips ghost across her skin. "I've been wanting to do that since the moment I saw you."

"Why didn't you?"

"Thought it'd be a weird way to say hello."

She playfully bats at my chest, removing herself from my lap as she searches for her clothes. We reach for her lacy black underwear at the same time, but I get there first, fisting the garment as I tuck it into my breast pocket. "Archie," she warns. "I need my underwear, you menace."

"These are mine now." She rolls her eyes as I tuck myself back into my jeans. "Get dressed Rosie girl, or we're gonna be goin' for round two."

Chapter 24

Archie

♫ *Santa Claus is Comin' To Town - Frank Sinatra*

"Hand me that wreath, would ya, Lottie girl?"

She's bundled up in her winter coat, the fresh blanket of snow covering our street leaving us nowhere to go and not much else to do but prepare for the holiday. Lottie's been itching to get outside, but Ro's been working on a new recipe. so I offered to bring her out with me while I put up Mama's Christmas decorations.

She passes me the wreath, pushing onto her tiptoes to reach me on the ladder. "Thanks, darlin'. How're you likin' Oak Ridge?"

"I love it!" she says, bounding down the porch steps to play in the snow once more. I glance back at the girl who looks so much like her mama as she falls back into the fresh powder, waving her arms and legs back and forth in a sweeping motion. "It's pretty here. And Mama said maybe we could get a dog."

"Did she now? What kinda dog would you like?"

She shrugs then lays there motionless. "Umm... Archie? How do I get up now?" she asks.

I laugh, carefully making my way down the ladder. "Stay there. I'm comin' to getcha." Once I get within a foot of her snow angel, she raises her arms, beckoning me to pull her up. I take her mittened hands in mine and pull. "Don't move your feet just yet," I tell her before adding, "I'm gonna lift you up if that's okay. That way we don't mess up your hard work." She nods and I place both hands under her armpits and lift her out of the snow, depositing her on the walkway I shoveled early this morning.

"What do you think?" she asks.

"Lookin' good, kiddo." We stand there for a minute, quietly admiring her creation.

"Hey Archie?"

"Hmm?"

"Catch me if you can," she says, right before a massive snowball hits me in the face, leaving me momentarily stunned. She darts away as fast as her little legs will carry her.

"Now you've done it," I say, letting her get a head start as she rounds the back of the house, pausing to make another snowball. I bend down to make a pile of my own, tossing one just shy of her position near the back porch. "You better run, Lottie girl!" I tease.

She tosses another, hitting me in the chest, and I have to admit she's got a pretty good arm for a kid her age. Her giggles echo around the yard as we make chase for what feels like hours, our fingers and toes numb by the end of our game when we slump down on the front porch. "You win," I concede. "You're too fast for this old man."

"What's that smell, Mama?" Lottie asks as she waltzes into the kitchen, red-faced and disheveled.

"Gingerbread pancakes. You wanna try one?" Lottie grimaces, and Rosie's face falls before she replaces it with her usual smile.

"Smells like heaven in here. Got enough for me, Ro? I'd love to try one!"

She hums along to White Christmas as she puts together two plates piled with stacks of pancakes smothered in whipped cream and butterscotch syrup. "Trust me," she says, sprinkling the top with crushed pecans. Her hips sway as she brings the dishes over to the eat-in kitchen, setting them down on the round table.

I exaggerate a moan around my first bite, giving Rosie a wink. "So good. But you know what? I don't know if I can finish it all." Lottie eyes my plate, and I know I've almost won her over. I take another bite, this time with extra toppings. The flavors mix on my tongue and this time the moan is involuntary. "It really is delicious, Ro. You should open your own restaurant."

She waves me off with a smile. "I don't know about all that," she says. But I didn't miss the longing in her eyes as she peered into the old boarded up bakery yesterday. She's exactly what this town needs, and I just have to figure out how to convince her.

After a few more bites. I subtly push my plate over to Lottie and, without a word, I stand to pluck another fork from the silverware drawer and place it beside the plate. Lottie hesitates slightly, as if weighing whether she wants to give us the satisfaction of her trying something new, or continue to be stubborn as a mule.

I decide for her. "If you don't like it, you can spit it out. I'll even hold out my hand for you." And I do. Lottie smiles, stabbing the fork into the side of the pancakes and scooping up some of the toppings. Rosie watches on bated breath as Lottie brings the fork to her mouth. Sure enough, I've got a palm full of gingerbread pancakes not 10 seconds later. "Alright, well. We tried," I chuckle, wiping my hand on a napkin. "You did good, kid." I offer my other hand in a high five as I smirk at Rosie across the table. She's got hearts in her eyes as she glances towards her daughter.

"Can I be excused?" With a nod from her mama, Lottie bounds up the stairs to her room as I help Rosie clear the table. The task is so domestic it almost feels like we've been doing this for years. Rolling up my sleeves, I start to wash the dishes as she leans against the counter with a dish towel, ready to dry each one.

The warm water is nothing compared to the heat thrumming through my veins. I almost can't stand to be this close to Rosie without feeling the urge to pull her to me and kiss her senseless.

In an attempt to divert the blood rushing south, I fill the silence. "Does Lottie still believe in Santa?" I ask.

She takes the wet plate from my hand, her eyes narrowed. "'Course. Why do you ask?"

"Well, Saturday's your first day workin' with me at the shop, and it just so happens to be the day that my Pops is dressin' up like Santa to take pictures with the kids. Thought Aunt Bea might be able to bring her down for a visit."

"Really? Sully agreed to that?"

I snort, handing her another dish. "It was his idea. But if I'm bein' honest, I think he just wanted to feel useful. He's still getting used to giving up control of the shop."

"That must've been hard," she says, laying the dish towel on the counter as she turns to face me. "For both of you, I imagine."

"It was. But not for the reasons you'd think. I was more than ready to take over. But Pops — he's had a rough go of it.

Doc wanted him to stay in the hospital another week, but he signed the paperwork for early discharge and that was that."

She steps into my space then, and I involuntarily place my hands on her round hips. Her arms skate around my neck, pulling me down for a chaste kiss. "Wish I had been here for you," she whispers against my lips. It's hardly more than a friendly declaration, but it feels much more significant.

"Wish you'd been here for all of it. Every second of the last 10 years. Always imagined we'd have this someday, but somewhere along the way I stopped hopin'."

With every word she pulls be impossibly closer. Her breasts push up against my chest, my growing erection pressing into her soft belly eliciting a strangled groan from deep within my chest. "Careful, Ro. Don't think you realize how much I want to bend you over this counter right now."

Her breath hitches and pupils dilate, telling me she's not so unaffected either. My heart is damn near beating out of my chest, for her — always for her. "But Lottie's upstairs so I can't do that, can I?" Ever so gently, my hands slide around the dip of her waist and around her back, teasing the exposed skin in the space where her blouse has separated from her skirt. "But one day I will. I'll have your dress hitched up above your ass, my face buried between your thighs — keepin' you on the edge, and you'll be begging to come on my tongue."

"Archie..." she breathes out my name like a prayer, our lips barely a hair's breadth apart.

"You want that, darlin'? Want my mouth on you? Tastin' you? Tell me."

"I want that," she says, her words barely audible if it weren't for the stillness in the room, our mingled breaths the only sound filling the silence.

"Mama! My tooth is loose!" Rosie jumps back at the sound of her daughter's voice echoing down the staircase, followed closely by the thump of tiny footsteps carrying into the kitchen.

I round the table, hiding my arousal behind a kitchen chair as Rosie crouches down beside Lottie. "You're right. Looks like you'll be down one tooth before we know it. Think Santa might bring you a new one?"

"That's silly, Mama! Santa doesn't bring teeth."

"Well, maybe you could ask him when we visit him this weekend."

Lottie's mouth drops open as the words register. "We're going to see Santa?" Her excitement is infectious and I find myself unable to hold back my grin.

"Yes, ma'am. I confirm. You're gonna meet me and your mama at the shop so *we* can get your picture taken with Santa. How does that sound, kiddo?" *We.* I hadn't meant to say it, but damn, did it feel so right.

Lotties squeals and launches herself at me. "I can't wait!"

The embrace catches me off guard, but I return the hug all the same and I think I fall a little in love with Lottie then. They almost feel like a vital part of me — one I intend to hold on to with both hands.

Chapter 25

Rosie

♫ *I Saw Mommy Kissing Santa Claus - The Ronettes*

I stare at the photo stuck to the fridge with a snowman magnet — the smile on Lottie's face is bigger than any I've seen since her Mamaw's passing. Archie did that. I know he would never take credit for it, but his presence has made a world of difference, for Lottie and for me.

Aunt Bea's voice snaps me out of my thoughts as I bring a steaming mug of coffee to my lips, hiding my wistful expression. "Love looks good on you, Ro."

Love. Is that what this is?

Of course it is. There's no denying it now. I don't think I ever stopped loving Archie Sullivan. From the moment I stepped foot in his mama's kitchen, I knew there would be no going back. My heart belongs to him, fiercely and irrevocably. I just have to find a way to stay.

"Did you hear from the lawyers about Mama's estate?"

Aunt Bea's shoulders slump and I brace myself for what comes next. "It's not good news, I'm afraid. Your daddy's

149

come outta the woodwork claiming this house belongs to him and any money she left for you and Lottie."

Tears gather along my lashes as I think about losing this house and everything along with it. She always wanted to come back here. For me and Lottie to have a home in the town she loved with the people she adored. "H-how can he do this? Where has he been for 10 years?"

"That's still a mystery to me, Rosie girl. I wish I had the answers. All I can tell you is we're gonna fight for you. Me and Uncle Chuck will be here as long as you need us. And when you're settled, we'll head back to Georgia," she says, glancing out the front window. "Everything'll be alright, my girl. And it looks like we're leaving you in expert hands."

I follow her line of sight, finding Archie on the front porch with a toolbox, straightening some of the loose spindles. "He's a good one," she adds.

"The best."

I step out onto the front porch, the cool December air stealing my breath as the scent of coffee mingles with the earthy smell left behind by the melting snow.

"Well, aren't you a sight for sore eyes," Archie says from his crouched position near the railing. His gaze flicks to the holiday mug in my hand. "That for me?"

"That depends. Can you afford it?" I tease, holding the mug away from his outstretched hand.

He stands, pushing into my space. "What's it gonna cost me?" he asks, his voice deep and rich, sending a pulse straight between my thighs.

"A kiss."

He plucks the cup of coffee from my grip, placing it carefully on the small table near the door. "Think I can manage that," he smirks. "Just one?"

I nod as he pushes me up against the siding, gently touching his forehead to mine. My heartbeat speeds up on contact, his cold palm reaching out to cup my warm cheek, causing me to wince. "Sorry, darlin'. Gonna need you to warm me up."

I open my mouth to respond, but before I can utter a single word, his lips are on mine. It's soft and unhurried, as though we have all day to sink into each other — a lifetime even — and I want that. So much.

"Ewww. Mama!" Archie chuckles against my lips as Lottie steps onto the porch, interrupting our heated exchange.

"Mornin', Lottie girl," he says, tapping her on the nose. "What can we do for ya?"

She looks at me expectantly and when I don't respond, she huffs. "You promised pancakes for breakfast! And not the yucky kind."

I smile affectionately at my 7-year-old. "You're right, my girl. I sure did. You wanna help me make 'em?" She bounces on her feet at the idea, nodding energetically.

"Wish I could bottle some of that energy for m'self," Archie says with a smirk.

I squeeze his hand, extracting myself from between him and the siding. "Join us for breakfast?"

"You don't hafta ask me twice. I'll just finish up here and meet y'all inside."

As Lottie flips the last pancake, Archie strolls into the kitchen, looking like every woman's fantasy. His hair looks mussed from pushing his hand through it, and I can't help but imagine what it would feel like to have that beard scratching between my thighs. *Rein it in, Ro.*

"Smells delicious in here," Archie says, not doing anything

to ease the ache that's building beneath my skirt. "And I'm starving." His heated gaze lands on me as I plate the last pancake.

"Go on into the living room and get Aunt Bea and Uncle Chuck for me, would ya, Lottie?."

As Lottie leaves the kitchen, Archie takes two plates from my hands, leaning in for a kiss — the act is so domestic it sends a jolt of longing through me. This. This is what I've been waiting for. A home. A family. I just hope I can keep it.

"Well, isn't this cozy?" a distantly familiar voice says from the doorway. Archie stiffens as he places the plates on the table, pulling me into his side.

"What do you think you're doing here, Bobby?" Aunt Bea says, stepping into his path.

My father takes several steps into the kitchen, pushing past my aunt with a scowl on his face. "I'm here to get what's mine," he says, his eyes bouncing between me and Archie. "This house belongs to me."

It's Uncle Chuck who speaks next. "You'll have to take that up with the lawyers. None of us have seen hide nor hair of your in 10 years. We don't owe you a damn thing."

It's my turn to speak now. "You left, daddy. Like a goddamn coward, you ran and left Mama to raise me all on her own. And now you want to come back here and take away the only thing I have left of her?" I'm on a roll now, letting loose 10 years' worth of anger. Archie's grip on my waist tightens. "You don't get to just walk back into my life and tear it to shreds like you did all those years ago. You ruined everything for me. I had a life here. Friends. A boyfriend."

"Looks to me like you've still got all of that, Rosie girl."

"Don't call me that. You don't ever get to call me that. Get the fuck out."

Archie releases his hold on me, kissing my temple tenderly

before stepping around the table. "You heard her, Bobby. Get out before we call the police."

Dad scoffs. "Go ahead, boy. They won't do a damn thing because my name is on the deed and it belongs to me."

"Bobby, just go. You've done enough damage," Aunt Bea says. With one last look at the four of us, my father stalks out of the room, slamming the screen door in his wake. It's only then that I notice the tiny figure cowering behind Uncle Chuck.

"Lottie, come here, please." She rushes over, clinging to my legs when she reaches me. I crouch down to her level. "Are you ok, sweet girl?"

She nods, but her tear-stained cheeks betray her. Archie approaches, sinking down beside me. "Hey kiddo, you wanna sit beside me and have some pancakes?"

She glances up at him, and her expression changes in an instant as she nods. Without an ounce of hesitation, he lifts her into his arms and sets her down at the table with a kiss on her head, like he's been doing it for years — like she belongs to him.

Archie gestures for me to sit on his other side. "You too, love. Can't have you witherin' away on me." *Love.* He's never called me that before. And I don't hate it. In fact, I think I might cherish it, cherish *him.*

Chapter 26

Archie

♫ *Santa Baby - Eartha Kitt*

Closing up the shop is like second nature, but it's vastly improved in the weeks since Rosie started working here. The lights are out on Main Street, only the soft glow of the street lamps lighting the road. I watch her gorgeous figure move around the shop as she sweeps the floor, her hips swaying to the Christmas carols playing over the radio. I switch off the overhead lighting, leaving only the warm Christmas lights lining our windows. As she nears the checkout counter, I cage her in with my body, my hips pressing her against the surface. "Remember what I told you the last time I had you like this?"

My hand skates along the back of her thigh, tugging up her long skirt. Stunned, she turns her head to meet my gaze. "Think I need a reminder," she says, her words breathy as she pushes her hips into my erection.

"Be a good girl and bend over for me, Ro." She places the broom to the side of the register before leaning her breasts over the weathered wood countertop. "That's my girl," I say, my hand pressing into her lower back. "So damn beautiful."

Rosie's breathing picks up as I expose her backside, rucking up her skirt and sliding her panties down her thick thighs. "Spread your legs for me, love."

She follows every command I give her without question, and fuck if that doesn't have my cock rock hard and straining beneath my jeans. I sink to my knees behind her, spreading her ass as I prepare for a feast. Her pretty pink pussy glistens at her apex, letting me know just how much my words affect her. "You like being told what to do?" It's not really a question. I have my answer the moment I slide my finger through her wetness and she moans.

"You'll come when I say, and not a moment before. Got it?"

She nods against the countertop. "Words, Ro. Or you won't get my tongue."

"Yes. God. Yes."

I tilt her hips further back, exposing more of her silky thighs and the treasure that hides between them. I glide my tongue along her center, her thighs shaking on contact. "Fuck. You taste even better than I imagined." I lick her again, this time applying more pressure with my tongue. My teeth graze her clit, causing her body to shudder as a mewl escapes her lips. "You like that?"

"Yes," she breathes. "Please."

Her pleading tone has me doubling my efforts, feasting on her pussy like a man starved. Nipping, sucking, licking, until she's writhing and bucking into me as I spread her wide. "You wanna come, darlin'? Ready to soak my face?"

She can't speak, each stuttered breath telling me I have her right where I want her. I tease her entrance with two of my fingers, and she pushes back, seeking more. "Greedy girl," I chuckle. "Your pretty pussy is begging to be filled, huh? You want my fingers or my cock?"

She stifles a moan but doesn't answer. "You better tell me, Ro, or you won't get to come."

"Please," she rasps. I glance at her face. Her eyes are unfocused, cheeks reddened and forehead slick.

"My girl is so needy. But you won't get what you want until you say the words. Say you want my cock and I'll give it to you."

She cries out as I suck hard on her clit, plunging two fingers into her soaking wet pussy, stroking inside. "I want your cock," she screams.

"Good girl."

With one hand still stroking in and out, I unbuckle my belt, freeing my impossibly hard cock. "I've been dreaming of you like this since that first day you started working here. Damn inconvenient to be picturing my girl bent over the counter when I'm tryin' to load up some lumber for a customer."

She laughs, but it's strained as I pull my hands away, lining myself up at her entrance. "Gonna be hard and fast. I won't last long. Not with your taste still on my tongue."

Before she can respond, I plunge balls deep into her, our hips flush against each other as I fuck her into the counter. Her pussy pulses around my length, strangling the life out of me. "So goddamn tight. I'll never get enough. You were made for me." With each word, she moans and cries out for more.

"That's it, love. Take it all. You own me." My fingers dig into her hips with each thrust. She glances over her shoulder, her hair cascading down her back in gold waves, exposing her neck.

Leaning over, I graze my teeth along the spot behind her ear, causing a shudder to roll through her body. With my lips against her ear, I whisper, "Come for me, love." And as though she'd been waiting ages for permission, she dissolves into pleasure, her eyes rolling back in her head as her pussy convulses around me.

I continue thrusting through her orgasm, electricity thrumming through my veins until I topple over the edge, spilling my release against her ass and thighs.

I smooth a hand down her spine. "Are you okay?" I ask, making sure she's not hurt in any way. I wasn't exactly gentle with her.

"Better than okay," she says with a laugh.

She tries to straighten, but I hold her down. "Wait. I need to get you cleaned up first."

I pull up my pants, realizing neither of us were fully undressed, despite one of the hottest experiences of my goddamn life. I head into the back room, returning with a wet cloth. Once she's clean, I replace her underwear and pull down her skirt. "Thank you," she says, wrapping her arms around my neck. "But now I think you owe me a kiss, seeing how I didn't get one in all of that excitement."

"You're right. How could I be so careless?" I snicker, taking her mouth in a deep, soul-crushing kiss.

"Let's go home," she whispers.

Home.

Chapter 27

Archie

♫ *Baby it's Cold Outside - Dean Martin*

Christmas Eve, 1967
Rosie and Archie, Age 15

Christmas carols play over the radio as Mama places two steaming mugs of hot cocoa on the coffee table in front of me and Rosie. *"Careful now, it's hot."*

"Thank you, Mrs. Sullivan." Rosie says, putting the finishing touches on her homemade Christmas ornament.

"You're welcome, dear. Holler if you need anything." Mama gives me a wink before striding out of the living room, leaving me alone with the girl of my dreams.

"Ro?"

"Hm?" she hums around a candy cane.

I'm glad her attention is focused elsewhere as I steady myself to ask the question I've been dyin' to ask for months. My palms

are sweaty and my knee is shaking uncontrollably. "Will you...
uh — will you be my girlfriend?"

Her eyes snap up to meet mine as she drops an entire bottle of
glitter on the living room rug. "Oh my god, I'm so clumsy."

She bends to pick it up, but I stop her, not wanting to wait
for her answer. "Leave it, darlin'. I'll have Mama get the
vacuum."

"Ok," she breathes. Silence stretches between us, my heart
beating out of my chest as I wait for her to continue speaking.
Her hand reaches out to mine, threading our fingers. The touch
sends sparks shooting up my arm. "Yes."

"Yes?"

"I'll be your girlfriend... on one condition." There's a hint of
mischief behind her smile and I want to kiss her senseless. But
I'm not sure if we're ready for that. I've never kissed anyone
before — if I'm bein' honest, I was waitin' for the girl next door
to notice me. And now that she has, I need to wait for the right
moment.

A smile breaks out across my face. "Name it. Whatever you
want."

"You have to admit that I make a better pecan pie than
Anita's Bakery."

A laugh startles out of me, as I pull her in for a quick hug.
"Was that even a question? 'Course you do! You make the best
damn pecan pie I've ever had."

"Language, Archie Sullivan!" Mama calls, her voice
carrying through the open doorway to the kitchen.

"Sorry Mama," I holler, winking across the couch at Rosie.
"Can you bring the vacuum in here?"

"You got two feet and a heartbeat, boy. Get it your damn
self."

"Language, Mama," I shoot back. Rosie giggles and the
sound makes my heart skip a beat. Does she know I'm already
halfway in love with her? Have been since we rode bikes together

159

at age 9. And even more so when she sat behind me in social studies, passing me notes with smiley faces on them. But what really did it was the cupcake she brought me on my birthday last year. It had a single candle, and she told me to make a wish. I wonder if she knows I've wished for the same thing every year since we met — Rosie Beaumont.

Mama strides into the room with a scowl on her face, a vacuum in hand, and we get the glitter explosion cleaned up in no time. Rosie's face scrunches as she carefully threads a red ribbon through her sparkly ornament. "There," she says. "Where should I hang it?"

She moves to stand, but I grip her wrist and pull her back down to the sofa. "Wait. Did you sign it?"

"No, why?"

"Every artist signs their work. Give it here."

She passes it to me, our fingers lightly brushing. With a pen in hand, I quickly scribble on the back, then place it in her upturned palm. "There. Now it's perfect."

Her brow furrows for a moment before she glances up at me through her lashes with a sweet smile. "Rosie Sullivan, huh?"

"Someday," I whisper.

Winter, 1979

Ever since the run-in with her father, I've been doin' everythin' I can to give Rosie a reason to stay. Although I'd love to say that bein' with me is enough to keep her here for good, I'm not naïve enough to believe that. But I think I've finally figured out the perfect plan.

Bright and early Monday morning, I walk into the kitchen to the smell of fresh coffee. "Mornin' Pops. Can I get the number for the real estate lawyer you worked with last year?"

"Sure. Is there a reason you need it?"

Grabbing a mug from the cupboard, I pour myself a cup, leaning back against the counter as my dad waits for my answer. I don't know why I'm nervous about sharing my plan. Suppose I don't want anyone to talk to me out of it.

"Found a piece of property I'm thinkin' about buyin'." I purposely keep the details vague. Dad knows I've been saving up to buy a house so I could get out of their hair now that he's stable and mostly recovered from the accident, so it wouldn't be a surprise that I'm looking at properties.

A genuine smile lights his face as he pulls a business card from his wallet and sets it on the counter. "Yeah? That's great, Arch. Proud of you, son."

"Thanks, Pops."

An hour later, I'm walking through the door to Sully's Hardware, with a little more pep in my step as I take in the sight of Rosie behind the counter in a pair of figure hugging jeans and a white blouse with the top 2 buttons undone. She's chatting it up with Marty Barlow — one of my regulars. "Hey darlin'," I say, leaning over to kiss her on the cheek. Normally I wouldn't be so affectionate in front of the customers, but something's telling me to stake my claim, even though Marty has a wife at home and a baby on the way. She's smiling at whatever he's sayin, and I wish I could keep all of that happiness for myself.

"Hey, Marty. Here for your lumber?" I ask, recalling the large order waiting in the lot for Barlow Construction. "I can meet you out back if you pull your truck 'round and we can get you loaded up."

"Sounds good, Arch." Turning his attention back to Rosie for a minute he says, "Nice to meet ya, doll. I'll be seein' you." With a wink, he's out the front door.

"What the hell was that?" Rosie says, swatting at my chest.

"Just makin' sure he knows you're my girl," I say, placing my hands around her back to pull her into me. She rolls her eyes but doesn't pull away so I lean in for a kiss, just a soft brush of her lips but it still feels like heaven. "I'll be right back."

When I get back from loading up Marty's order, Rosie is busy with another customer, so I slip into the back office and pull out the business card. "Here goes nothin'."

Chapter 28

Rosie

♫ All My Christmases - Jillian Edwards

Archie's been acting strange since our tryst at the hardware store, and I don't know what to make of it. He's not distant exactly, but he's been spending a lot of time in the office, taking phone calls. Eavesdropping feels like an invasion, but I need answers, so I'm planted outside the office door, keeping an eye on the till as his hushed voice echoes through the back room. "I don't care what it costs, Jim. Drain the account for all I care." I can't quite make out the voice on the other end of the line, and I don't recall having heard of anyone named Jim in recent memory. "Yes, I'm sure. Whatever it takes. Yes. Thanks. I'll come by tomorrow."

At the click of the phone, I rush back to the front just in time as Archie strides up behind me, kissing my cheek. "Everythin' good out here?"

"Yep. All under control, boss," I tease.

"Mmmm. Careful, love. Calling me boss is really doin' it for me."

163

"Get a room, you two." I glance up to see Elanor walking into the store with a box under one arm. "Got the last of the decorations for your tree. Can't believe you waited 'til the last minute to enter the contest."

"It's all her fault," he jokes. "I didn't want to enter in the first place, but she's very convincing."

She snickers, giving us a knowing look. "I'll bet she is. You be sure to keep him in line, Rosie girl."

"I'll do my best, Mrs. S."

"Pfft. You call me Mama, now. We'll be family sooner or later. I'll see y'all for dinner. Don't be late." And with that, she disappears out the door without another word.

Plucking the box off the counter, I head over to the 6ft artificial tree we've erected in the shop window. It's barren except for a few strands of colorful lights and a handful of glass ornaments. I dig through the box, pulling out several ropes of tinsel garland, a set of silk wrapped balls, and an old angel tree topper that I recognize from years ago. Near the bottom of the box, I find a small package wrapped in tissue. I carefully pull it out, unwrapping the delicate paper as glitter falls to the floor. When the sparkly star shaped ornament comes into focus, all the air whooshes from my lungs. "He kept it." I whisper.

"Of course I did." I didn't even hear him approach and my vision blurs as I flip the ornament over, tracing the messy scrawl on the back that reads "Rosie Sullivan."

"Why?" I ask. "After all this time?"

"I loved you then, and I love you now. And every moment in between." He sits beside me on the floor, pulling me onto his lap. "I've always loved you, Rosie. Whether your last name is Beaumont or Sullivan, I will love you until my last breath."

I close my eyes, resting my head against his chest, feeling his heartbeat beneath my palm. "I love you, too." The tears I worked so hard to keep at bay escape down my cheeks, soaking his plaid button down. His hand traces patterns along my spine, soothing the ache left behind by 10 years apart.

The bell chimes above the door, breaking us from our tender embrace. "Better get back to work," he says, as I push up from the floor. With one more sweet kiss, he heads back to the counter and I'm left clinging to the last thread of hope that we can find a way to stay.

"I'm home!" I call into the entry as I hang up my winter coat.

"Hey, Ro." Aunt Bea says, a solemn expression on her face. "Come sit down, honey."

She leads me into the living room where I find Uncle Chuck sitting with a pile of papers on the coffee table, his elbows resting on his knees, head hanging between his shoulders.

"I'm so sorry." The words echo through the quiet space, stealing the air from my lungs.

"No," I murmur. "Tell me it's not what I think."

"I'm afraid it is, my girl. We have to be out of the house by New Year's Eve. Your dad retains the deed and everything that was here before we arrived."

If it weren't for the arms that band around my waist, I would've collapsed to the floor, my body wracked with uncontrollable sobs. "Breath, love," Archie whispers, holding me upright. "We'll find a way to fix this. I promise." He sinks down on the couch, bringing me with him.

"We'll give you some time," Aunt Bea says, leading Uncle Chuck out of the living room.

"What are we gonna do?" I sob.

Archie's hand strokes down my hair, holding me tightly as

the tears begin to slow. "We'll take this one day at a time. If we can't find some place for you to live, you'll come stay with me. I'm not losin' you again, Ro. I can't do it. My heart wouldn't survive it."

"What about Lottie? There isn't enough space in your house for all of us."

"We'll figure it out. If I have to sleep on the couch, so be it. If I have to move into the office at the shop, I'll sleep on the goddamn floor. I don't care what it takes. I'm not losin' either of you. For now, let's just get through the holiday."

"Ok," I sigh. We stay like that for a while, his arms around me, holding me against him in a comforting embrace.

Once the tears have dried, he palms my cheek, bringing his lips to my forehead. "Go get cleaned up. Mama's waiting on us for dinner and I don't much wanna find out what happens if we're late."

Chapter 29

Rosie

♫ *Wrapped Up in You - Dolly Parton*

Walking down Main Street on Christmas Eve, I shove my mitten clad hands into the pockets of my threadbare jacket, the midday sun casting shadows on the buildings is not enough to warm my frozen fingertips and toes. I stop in at the flower shop to pick up a bouquet for Mama E's Christmas centerpiece, saying a quick hello to Betty before heading back out into the frigid air. She chatted me up for a spell as I congratulated her for winning the tree decorating contest, to absolutely no one's surprise.

I almost stroll past the boarded up bakery when my eyes snag on the sold sign in the window. Something like sadness sinks into my chest, but it doesn't have a chance to grow before a pair of strong arms envelope me from behind. "Hey beautiful," Archie murmurs. "Fancy meetin' you here."

I turn in his hold, melting into him with a deliciously slow kiss. "Miss me?" I tease.

"Always, darlin'. You got everythin' you need?"

I hold up my shopping bags and the bouquet of roses and carnations so much like the ones Archie picked out several weeks ago. "All set."

"Good. I'm starvin' and Mama's cookin' up a feast."

"Can I help with anything?" I ask, placing the last stem into the crystal vase in the center of the dining table.

Elanor smiles as she pulls the turkey out of the oven. "I've got it all under control, dear. You go on into the living room and see what your kiddo is up to. I'll call ya when dinner's ready." There's something in her expression that tells me she knows more than she's letting on.

A high-pitched squeal carries through the hallway followed by a chorus of giggles. When I round the corner into the living room, I catch sight of my girl rolling around on the floor with a little white ball of fluff. Archie smirks at me from his spot on the sofa, patting the seat beside him.

I approach with my hands on my hips. "Archie Sullivan. What did you do?"

"Mama! Look! Archie got a puppy!"

"I can see that." I grit my teeth, muttering the next part under my breath for only Archie to hear. "Tell me you didn't get Lottie a puppy."

"I would, but that'd make a liar outta me."

He tugs on my hand, pulling me onto his lap. His breath fans over my ear, sending tingles up my spine. "She doesn't know it's hers yet. If you don't want her to have it, it'll be mine. But look at that smile and tell me it's not worth it."

I glance back at my daughter, who's grinning from ear to

168

ear as the pup chases its tail around in a circle. I let out a resigned sigh. "Is it a boy or a girl?"

"It's a boy," he replies. "Lottie girl, did you think of a name for him?"

"Hmmm..." she scrunches her nose in concentration, eyeing the little guy as he jumps into her lap and makes himself at home. "What about Snowball? He's all fluffy and white. And it's almost Christmas after all."

"That sounds great to me, kiddo. Whaddaya think, Ro?" I nod in agreement, a smile tugging at my lips.

"She's happy," I sigh. "Thank you."

"You don't have to thank me. I'm just happy to have y'all here."

"Rosie girl. Good to see ya," Sully says, leaning heavily on his cane before sinking into his armchair across from my spot on Archie's lap. I feel a little awkward, so I attempt to move, but Archie holds me in place and Sully gives me a knowing grin.

"Arch, did you get in touch with the lawyer?" I feel him stiffen behind me and I wonder, not for the first time, what kind of secrets Archie is keeping from me. This time I do manage to slip off his lap, taking up a spot on the floor beside Lottie and Snowball.

"I did. Thanks Pops." He's being tight-lipped about something and it's getting under my skin. I eye him warily, absent-mindedly stroking a hand through soft fur. His expression gives nothing away, and I'm left with more questions than answers.

"Dinner's ready!" Elanor calls just as Aunt Bea and Uncle Chuck arrive at the door. "Perfect timing. Come on in," she says. After hanging their coats on the hooks, we all proceed into the dining room where the table is set with the wedding china and a feast fit for a king.

"Wow, Mama. This looks amazing." Archie kisses her on

the cheek before pulling out a chair and gesturing for me to sit.

"Such a gentleman," I tease.

He leans down to whisper in my ear, just loud enough for me to hear. "I think we both know I'm not." I clench my thighs to dull the ache as he slides into the chair beside me, laying a possessive arm around my shoulder. Snowball circles the table, finding a spot at Lottie's feet where he sits back on his haunches, awaiting the scraps that my daughter will no doubt pass him when she thinks we're not looking.

The meal is every bit as delicious as I expected, and the company is even better. I can't remember the last time I felt so at ease — probably before Mama got sick. It only solidifies how much I need to stay in Oak Ridge. It's like it's written in the stars and I can't stand the thought of leaving all of this behind.

Archie

By the time Rosie brings out her famous pecan pie, I'm practically salivating — and not just for the pie. Rosie looks delicious in her flowy green skirt and floral blouse with her golden hair flowing around her shoulders in waves.

I almost lost my mind when Pops nearly spilled the beans before the grand reveal. I don't know what I woulda done if the truth had come out before I'm ready. I've spent the better part of a week dodging questioning glances from Rosie and avoiding anything to do with my secret phone calls.

Between the realtors, lawyers, movers, and cleaning crew, everything is ready for a Christmas reveal. I just have to keep everything under wraps until then. I'd hoped the puppy would be a big enough distraction, but Rosie's still eyeing me suspiciously as she places a slice of pecan pie on the table in front of me. "What are you up to, Archie Sullivan?"

"No idea what you're talking about, Rosie girl." I pull her into my lap, stab a corner of the pie and bring it to her lips. She moans around the bite, and the sound goes straight to my cock. I know she feels it straining against her backside as she wiggles her ass suggestively. "I'll get you for this later," I murmur.

"Looking forward to it." She smirks before removing herself from my lap. "Eat your pie," she says.

And I do. Every bite is like a memory; Rosie and me riding bikes down the drive. Rosie cheerin' me on from the stands at my track meet. Rosie curled up against my side watching a movie while I watched her instead. Every moment I thought long forgotten comes back to me as the sugary sweet flavors dance on my tongue. I can imagine the future, too, and damn, does it paint a pretty picture.

Mama and Bea shoo us from the kitchen, insisting on handling the dishes themselves.

"It's getting late," I say, glancing across the room at Lottie, who's curled up by the fire with a sleeping Snowball at her feet. "Why don't y'all stay the night? We can have Christmas morning here."

Rosie's eyes are heavy as she nods her agreement. I gently coax her onto a pillow, kissing her forehead. "I'll head over to the house with Uncle Chuck and bring everything here for Lottie, okay?"

I turn to leave, but before I get far, she clutches my wrist. "Arch?"

"Yeah, darlin'?"

"No matter what happens, I'm staying."

"Wasn't ever gonna let you go, Rosie girl. You're stuck with me."

Chapter 30

Rosie

♫ *Feels Like Christmas - Brett Eldridge*

The living room is a disaster with wrapping paper and bows strewn everywhere, an energetic Snowball rolling around in the mess. Christmas carols play softly over the radio as we watch Lottie play with her new toys, and I'm so distracted by the simplicity of the moment that I don't notice Archie placing something in my lap.

I glance down at the hand knit stocking, a perfect match to Archie's with my name embroidered along the top. "Did Mama E make this?"

Archie nods. "Look inside."

He watches me attentively as I reach into the stocking, my fingers wrapping around a velvet box. It feels too big to be a ring. Before I can open it, he places his hand over mine. "This is gonna change everything, Ro. I didn't do this lightly." He squeezes my hand before releasing his hold on me.

Without an ounce of hesitation, I pry open the box, revealing a small silver key. "Arch? What is this?"

"It's a key."

Unable to contain myself, my shoulders shake with laughter. "How does a key change everything?"

"Ready for an adventure, Rosie girl?" he says, pulling me up from the couch as he holds out an arm for my daughter. She takes his hand as he leads us out to the truck.

"Where are we going, Archie Sullivan?" My tone is dripping with false aggravation as he navigates the familiar streets of Oak Ridge, now glistening from the melting snow.

"Patience, love. We're almost there." He pulls onto Main Street and just when I think he's going to stop at the shop, he passes it by, parking outside the old boarded up bakery. "Stay there," he says, before hopping out of the driver's seat and rounding to my side. He reaches out a hand to help me down, then does the same for Lottie. Once we're standing on the sidewalk, the warm sun dulling some of the chill in the air, he holds out a hand for the key. I eye him curiously as I place it in his open palm.

My mind struggles to register each motion as he grips my hand and tugs me to the door of what used to be Anita's Bakery. What was once a part of the vibrant epicenter of Oak Ridge, is now empty — a shell of its former self, not unlike the woman I was just last year. But something changed when I came back, and maybe that means more than I'm willing to admit just yet.

Archie slides the key into the lock and, with a click, the door swings open. It's not as unkempt as I would have expected. Nor is it musty. The space is pristine, and it smells faintly of lemon. "Welcome home," he says, flicking on the overhead lights. But the words don't seem to hold any meaning as I scan the space.

The glass case that once held an array of pies and pastries gleams under the fluorescent lighting. The antique gold cash register still sits on the weathered wood countertop, and the

173

chalkboard beside the swinging doors to the kitchen has "Rosie's Diner" written in a messy scrawl that I would recognize anywhere.

It hits me all at once as tears gather along my lashes. Rosie's Diner. *My diner.*

"Archie —"

He cuts me off with a kiss, his hands cupping both of my cheeks as he wipes away the tears that are streaming down my cheeks. "It's yours. And when you're ready, there's more."

"More? How could there possibly be more than this? This. This is everything."

"No, darlin'. You are everything."

Lottie rushes over, wrapping her arms around my waist. "Why are you crying?"

I crouch down to her level, pulling her into a hug. "Mama's just happy, honey."

Pulling her up with me, I scan the space again with fresh eyes. It's all mine and I have so many big ideas. But first. "I'm ready for more."

Archie

The look on Rosie's face when she realizes what I've known for weeks now is well worth the wait. With Lottie on her hip, I guide her through the swinging doors to the kitchen, not stopping to show off the newly installed commercial oven as I head straight through the back to the set of hidden stairs.

As the narrow staircase comes into view, she places Lottie back on her feet and they follow me up into the apartment overhead. This is the space I spent most of my time working on, though it still needs Rosie's touch to make it truly feel like home. "It's 2 bedrooms and 2 baths. The living room is to your left with the big fireplace, and the kitchen is to your right. The bedrooms are down the hall. Each one has its own bathroom."

Lottie dashes off down the hallway in search of her room as Rosie's fingers trail the white kitchen countertops, her gaze snagging on the double oven along the far wall. But my eyes are fixed on her empty left hand.

Her smile lights up as she makes her away around the island to the expansive living room, freshly painted in a warm neutral until Rosie decides what she wants to do with it. There's a large velvet sofa in the center of the room, perfectly placed in front of a brick fireplace.

"This is amazing, Archie. I don't know what to say."

I reach into my pocket, fingering the dainty gold band with the marquis diamond in the center. With a steading breath, I hold the ring between us, an unspoken question hanging in the air. "Just say you'll stay."

She smiles then, and steps into my space, wrapping her arms around my waist as her lavender scent envelopes me. Her cheek rests on my chest, my steady heartbeat picking up as I wait for her response. "I'll stay," she murmurs. "Of course I'll stay."

Chapter 31

Rosie

♫ *Have Yourself a Merry Little Christmas - Dean Snowfield*

Present day

Archie and I are perched at our usual spot towards the end of the counter, sharing a slice of my famous pecan pie as the bell chimes above the door. I glance towards the entrance as Paige and Cade approach. She's got that pregnancy glow, and Cade reminds me of a younger Archie. There's this protectiveness radiating from him as he hovers a little closer than usual at his wife's side.

"Well hey there, my girl," Archie says, pulling Paige into a side hug. "Bet you're happy to be out and about after that storm. Haven't seen anything like it in years. 'Cept maybe that ice storm last year."

Cade shudders at the mention of last year's storm, and Paige giggles. "It wasn't so bad. Gave me some time to get a lot of baking done." She holds out an emerald green gift bag with a delicate ribbon, and I take it with a smile. I peek into the bag, catching a glimpse of the little snowflake like cookies she loves to make around the holidays.

"Oh, Paige! You are a ray of sunshine!" I say, pulling her in for a gentle hug. "These look delightful!"

"I had some help," she says, launching into a tale full of their adventures while they were snowed in at the cabin. Archie and I were lucky to get out after the second day, since the main roads weren't so bad. But those days we spent hunkered down above the diner were some of the best in recent memory. It took me right back to that first Christmas as a family, and shortly after, when I found out I was pregnant with Lottie's younger brother, AJ. We didn't have much back then, but I wouldn't change it for the world.

"Anyway, I thought everyone could use a little sweetness after being snowed in," Paige adds.

"Why don't y'all join us for brunch? I've got a stack of strawberry pancakes with your name on 'em. Might even have some fresh whipped cream."

"You had me at pancakes."

Archie

The Ridge looks like a Christmas wonderland as we step through the front doors. The bar is hardly recognizable beneath the string lights and greenery covering the wide open space. We're the first to arrive, save for Paige and Cade and their usual crew. I wave towards our hosts, pulling Rosie tight to my side. She's a vision in emerald this evenin', and I can't seem to keep my hands to myself. 45 years together and she still makes my heart skip a beat.

We pass Miles and Maggie locked in a staring contest, as we approach Paige and Cade near the buffet table. "You did good, kiddo." I say, pulling Paige in for a hug, her small baby bump protruding between us. "And how's the little one treating you?" I ask, thinking back on those early days when Rosie was pregnant with AJ and she could hardly keep any food down.

"Not so bad. If I didn't love them so much already, I'd be a lot more upset about the lack of pasta in my life these days. I'm basically existing on loaded baked potatoes and a prayer at this point."

"Try some ginger candies and saltines," I suggest. "Always worked for Ro."

Rosie looks up at me with a faint smile. "You remember that?"

"I remember everything', love." I lean down to place a chaste kiss on her painted red lips.

When I pull back, she smirks, swiping her thumb over my mouth. "Lipstick."

As the jukebox plays a familiar tune, I tug my wife onto the dance floor. With one hand on the dip of her waist, and her hand clasped in mine over my heart, I start to sway. "Have I told you lately how much I love you?"

"Archie Sullivan, are you flirtin' with me?"

"Always, Rosie Sullivan. Always."

Letters from Rosie to Archie

My dearest Archie,

It's been a week since we fled Oak Ridge, and each day I miss you more than the last. I wish I could tell you everything, but the truth is none of it matters in the end. Please understand that we left because we had to. Mama didn't leave me any other choice, and the man who was supposed to be my father has taken everything from me. I'm coming back to you, Archie. I don't know when, and I don't know how. Just know that I love you and I will return.

Love,
Rosie Beaumont

My dearest Archie,

There are so many things I wish I could say to you, but nothing feels adequate. My heart is aching and I feel empty inside where your love and friendship once made me whole. I dreamed we would one day grow old together, but with each passing day I fear we may never get that. You changed me, Archie. On some soul deep level, I will never be the same for having loved you. I will see you again. I swear it.

All my love,
Rosie Beaumont

My dearest Archie,

I hope this letter finds you well, though I am beginning to wonder whether my letters will ever make it to their destination. I've been gone for nearly a month now, and with every passing day this emptiness grows. I miss you, Archie.

I never knew what it was to miss a person until you. I wish I could tell you everything, just know I'm coming back. Come hell or high water, I will be in your arms again.

I love you now and I loved you then.
Yours forever,
Rosie Beaumont

My dearest Archie,

Mama says the letters aren't reaching you. I don't know why, and I'm saddened at the prospect that you may never know why I left. My only regret is that I didn't fight harder to see you that day — to say goodbye. I'll do everything I can to come back to you, my love. But it's selfish of me to wish you'd wait for me, so I won't. I hope you have a full life, Arch. You deserve the world. And maybe someday, I can be part of that.

Love always,
Rosie Beaumont

My dearest Archie,

Happy Anniversary, my love. It's been 45 years and my love for you has only grown stronger each day. We've faced many challenges in our long life together — we're no stranger to loss and to grief — but our love never wavered. There will come a day that I may have to go on without you, or you me, but I know when that day comes we will have been blessed beyond measure to have lived a life so full. My heart belongs to you, Archie. Fiercely and irrevocably.

Love always,

Rosie Sullivan

Acknowledgments

To my husband, thank you for never questioning the late nights and the lack of sleep. I love you.

To my 2 beautiful girls, once again, put the book down and back away slowly. I love you both to pieces.

To Cassandra, forever my Ivy. The first person to encourage me to write, and the first person to congratulate me when I finish. No, not like that, you slut. Love you to the moon.

To everyone who gave Oak Ridge a chance, even if you decided it was hot garbage, thank you for helping this baby author realize a long-held dream.

To Dreana, my indie author bestie and the one I run to when I need to complain, or have a good cry about this crazy journey we're on. Thank you for convincing me to finish these stories. It wouldn't have been possible without your incessant begging and vague threats. Someday we'll meet in the middle. Now go finish your book!

To my incredible team of alpha and beta readers, thank you for constantly listening to me complain about how difficult it was to finish this story. Thank you for loving Oak Ridge almost as much as I do.

To my family, friends, thank you for being the best support system anyone could ever hope for. This wouldn't be possible without each and every one of you.

Lastly, to YOU! If you're reading this, you now hold a tiny fraction of my heart in your hands. Thank you for reading!

About Willa

Mom of two humans and several cats, wife of 15 years, photographer, and professional over thinker. Willa has been an avid reader from a young age. As an angsty teen, she started using writing as an outlet for her big feelings. It took nearly 20 years to finally get up the courage to write her heart story — Heartstrings & Horizons. Ever since, she hasn't been able to stop writing.

Also by Willa Kay

Oak Ridge Series

Heartstrings & Horizons | Oak Ridge Book 1

Coming Soon

Moonlight & Matrimony | Oak Ridge Book 2

Deception & Daylight | Oak Ridge Book 3

Made in the USA
Columbia, SC
16 November 2024